INTERROGATIONS

Martin Ott

Fomite
Burlington, VT

ISBN-13: 978-1-942515-42-5
Library of Congress Control Number: 2015960526

Fomite
58 Peru Street Burlington, VT 05401
www.fomitepress.com

Cover art: Tolland #1 2010 © Judith Herron

Other Books by Martin Ott

Captive, De Novo Prize Winner, C&R Press
The Interrogator's Notebook, Story Merchant Books
Poets' Guide to America, written with John F. Buckley,
Brooklyn Arts Press
Underdays, Sandeen Prize Winner, University of Notre
Dame Press
Yankee Broadcast Network, written with John F. Buckley,
Brooklyn Arts Press

For my mother, whose love of books and reading is in my DNA. I can't look at a bookshelf without thinking of her.

"If you tell the truth, you don't have to remember anything."

– Mark Twain

CONTENTS

Acknowledgements

Beyond Baroque Magazine	Radio Radio
The Chaffey Review	Summer Snows
Cimarron Review	Stone Feathers
Connecticut Review	Mosquito Island
Fjords Review	The Diary Of Spidey-Bat
The Literary Review	Sugar, Wine, Smoke, and Glue
The Los Angeles Review	No One
Midwest Coast Review	Outside
Nimrod	Nick's Place
Pank Magazine	Vegas Everywhere I Go
Paradise Review	Gps Love Affair
Phoebe	Virgin Of The Parkway
Quality Paperback Literary Review	Intersection
Referential Magazine	The Interrogator's Last Question
The Southern California Anthology	Layover
Sou'wester	The Dancing Interrogator
Superstition Review	The Policy
Storyglossia	In The Dark
Terrain Magazine (Terrain.org)	Hunter's Point
Zone 3	Bulldog

No One

No one could make the bar crowd at the Pump House in Manley erupt quite the same way. No one could ring the bell mounted above the bins of scratcher tickets with quite so much gusto, and dole out a week's salary buying free shots for his audience of gold miners, roustabouts, and bush pilots. No one could encourage the few women to shimmy quite this wildly to a jukebox blasting Aerosmith and Lynyrd Skynyrd on a small stage set aside for open mike night. No one could high five quite like him, with two fingers, with one knee, with a dilapidated Goldpanners baseball cap, with the intensity of a man who made sure that all toasts within earshot were in his honor, and that all photos captured his unwashed blonde locks, intense Swedish eyes the sheen of dollar bills, and scraggly beard diving into frame.

No one had more cautionary tales about companions maimed or killed by the unforgiving wilderness, the death count often rising to a dozen by breakfast in the bar, usually consisting of hard boiled eggs, raw onions, and a double Bloody Mary. There were the usual fiery deaths from airplane crashes in inclement weather and in blazes from passed-out drunks, the disappearances from coastal storms and snowmobiles sinking in ice, the bear attacks and car crashes, limbs lost from four wheelers and Caterpillar blades, fingers shed from fishing line and husky bites, and the usual maiming from buck shot, oil burns, and chainsaws.

No one excelled at bar games with the same ferocity. No one could sling dice with a cunning fueled by a savant's innate understanding of statistics or foretell the bingo numbers, which were the birthdates of past girlfriends and wives. No one could draw a cue ball to the eight with perfect English or stick the final double on bar darts with a combination of daring and grace that made him the target of men and women alike.

No one could lie quite so extravagantly, with endless tales of tramping cross country as a teenager through the Louisiana bayou, or escaping his dull fate as an exiled Austrian prince, ducking the law from his stint as a high-end cat burglar in Asia and his tour as a medic in Iraq, with enigmatic tattoos to support each of the yarns, and with so much bare skin exposed in an evening that there were men who knew the markings of his body better than those of their children or wives.

No one else could destroy things with the flair of a human cyclone—frosted tumblers shattering and cue sticks cracking in bar fights, the automobiles and snow machines he "borrowed" plowed into snow banks and trees, the pretzel sticks he drunkenly swashbuckled in his fingers before devouring them, the hearts of wives and girlfriends breaking in his wake along with the knuckles of husbands on his rock of a head.

No one knew that he was not long for this world, and said so quite often, inhabiting each moment as though it were his last. Friends became enemies and then friends, his loves and his brawls were all intimately picked, the Northern lights in his eyes keeping the darkness licking at them at bay, a human torch to unsteadily lead the way.

No one disappeared as quickly as he came. He was and then wasn't with no signs of departure, his cabin still stocked and his screenless TV a shrine to the photos of women he'd left behind. He was a passenger to new places or else lost in the snow and eaten by wolves, or slain by jealousy or whisked away from love that caught fire, his meager possessions ceremoniously charred one by one in the Pump House fireplace, and the stories grew into legend, and the men and women grew old in each other's arms.

The Interrogator's Last Question

Navigating truth and lies is *a lot like driving someone else's car. Your job isn't to provide your passenger with a map, but to steer them over ruts, dry riverbanks, and intersections on lonely country roads to where it is you want to go.*

David had been an interrogator in the army for almost twenty years and knew how to ask questions that dug marrow from bone. Sometimes the questions were aimed at other people. He liked these best—the ones he asked himself never quite left his head, like sand in a pair of sneakers after a long walk on the beach. Like the voice rattling in his head: *Why do you find yourself driving around for hours after work instead of coming home?*

It was a good question, but didn't quite hit the mark—this was no rambling moonlit drive through the suburban subdivision sprawl he called home. David knew, for instance, that the moon was 5 days from new and that sunset would wake him at 5:36 tomorrow morning. The barometer was 29.8 and rising, the wind WSW, from 3 to 5 m.p.h. He also knew that no cherry trees grew on Cherry Lane, which he'd just turned onto, and that the needle of his gas tank had dipped below EMPTY 12.5 miles back, indicating that he had another 10 miles to spare.

Observation, which he'd once thought meant everything when interrogating prisoners, was now only good for estimating the amount of Glen Fiddich in a shot glass or the gas he needed to sputter into his driveway on vapors. He'd left his desk at Aries Consulting with a sore back and dry throat, downed a few at a nearby tavern, and exhausted a quarter tank stewing over his problems. His wife Liz—who worked as a trainer at the same firm—had already been home for hours. Plenty of time for her to get into trouble. Even during the best of times, which these, currently, were not.

It didn't surprise him to see a police car parked across his driveway and a pair of humorless officers talking to Liz, who motioned at them with a Frisbee as though she wanted to play catch. Next to her, their eldest son Raymond fidgeted in place as though he had to urinate, his expression wavering between amusement and shock as his pals watched from their open living room windows.

It looked as though another high school party at his house had spiraled out of control. David pulled over and got out, thinking about how Liz used to believe they were the coolest mother and father team. Now, only she was apparently. He just wished his home wasn't the party spot for D.C.'s most prestigious alternative high school. He walked up to the older of the officers, who shined a light in his face.

"All this over an innocent game," Liz said. "David, tell them I'm just hanging out with my teenage boys on a weekend night. That makes me a responsible mother."

David addressed the police calmly, in full damage control mode. "Sorry, officers, it's my fault. I was out playing poker with my friends and my wife is just trying to get attention by causing a scene."

"Son-of-a-bitch," Liz said.

"As you can see, I have a full evening ahead of me," David joked, gauging the cops' mouths, now quivering with smiles. "I'll take her in now and get my punishment," he said confidently, knowing he'd used the correct approach.

David took hold of Liz's arm. The officers laughed. She tore away from him and stomped inside, past Raymond and the teens peeking out on the front porch.

"Lots of kids here," the older officer said. "A lot of cars in your driveway."

"It's wrestling pay per view," David lied. "My wife gets a little worked up watching men in leotards."

The younger officer snorted and flicked off his light, following his partner to the squad car.

"I'll look after her," David called after the officers, knowing there was still a good chance he'd be seeing them later that evening.

Raymond shook his head and said, "Ever think that maybe this is your fault?"

The voice in David's head said, *Even your oldest, as selfish as he is, knows something is wrong here.* Raymond grew tired of waiting for a response and stormed back inside.

****** ****** ******

A flower is a worthy present for a wife, but it is encyclopedic for the interrogator. Days after it is picked, it begins falling apart, limb by limb. When it is parched and gasping for water, it is a thing of beauty as the truth strips away and falls into your hands.

In the flower boxes next to his house, David brushed past the rose bushes he'd once planted with Liz, when they both had the time and impulse for a hobby together. He reached in through the broken storm window of his den and unlatched it, crawling up over the ledge as he often did when he wanted to avoid the drunken kiddyfests in his living room.

His feet caught on the shades and he landed in an awkward shoulder roll on the carpeting, his feet rocking into his sturdy Korean War era filing cabinet. David flopped around like a turtle on his back before finally righting himself. His thirteen-year-old son Leo didn't even look up from the small television David kept there for the occasional sporting event. His youngest son was hanging out alone, paying rapt attention to an old Eroll Flynn and Bette Davis flick. Raymond's drunken friends razzed Leo, even when he tried to stay out from underfoot.

"Hey, kiddo, did you see the old man can still do a forward somersault?"

Leo smoothed his collar and said, "Hey, Dad," without looking up from the movie. Even though it was a Friday night, his son was wearing black slacks and a maroon tie draped over a long-sleeve shirt with buttoned cuffs. Most everyone on both sides of the family thought he might be gay and, while David didn't disagree, it didn't change the fact that Leo was by far the best adjusted person in the house.

"Have you seen your Mom?"

"No, not since she led limbo in the backyard," Leo said. "She might be upstairs. Asleep. Dancing on the roof. Whatever."

"What are you watching?"

"Do you care or are you just trying to make small talk?" Leo glanced up from the TV screen with dark brown humorless eyes that reminded him of his own.

"Son, don't be that way. I wanted to make sure—"

"I'm OK, Dad. Really. I just thought you might want to go check on Mom. She's been acting that way again.

"Of course, good night."

David pushed the den door into the hallway and was greeted by the yelps and barks of the living room speakers. His stomach gurgled from too many drinks with only an appetizer of fried mushrooms to coat them. A mass of kids controlled the living room and, he imagined, the adjoining game room. He glimpsed several silhouettes clutching plastic cups and smelled the cloying mixture of cigarettes, freshly baked brownies, and keg beer.

He slipped off his shoes and propelled himself toward the carpeted stairs. David trudged up them slowly, his life as much in turmoil as any teenager's. He ached to see Liz and yet there were things weighing on his mind that he, until recently, had been unable to voice. Even to himself. Liz was the only confidante he'd ever had in a lifetime of manipulative relationships, helping him to learn to trust his emotions instead of controlling them. The steps to the second floor seemed to go forever; his feet felt almost as heavy as his heart.

Down the hallway, Jim Madsen, a.k.a. Mad Dog, stood outside the bathroom, waiting to pee. Raymond's best friend chewed on an empty plastic cup and had an inane smile, one that David would undoubtedly see over hot cakes the next morning along with the dozen or so other teens too inebriated to make their way home. The bathroom door opened and Liz trailed out, an Aries T-shirt draped over a pair of aquamarine underwear.

David's heart caught in his throat when he saw his wife. Her presence made him reel in terror and helplessness as nothing else did. She had the same body she had twenty years ago, the same unflinching eyes. Mad Dog and Liz had difficulties passing each other in the narrow hall. Finally, Jim grabbed Liz's arm and pivoted around her toward the john. As the soccer striker and quiz bowl captain cleared his wife's curves, Liz cupped a hand between Mad Dog's legs before ambling down the hallway. Jim grunted in surprise, then teetered into the bathroom, bolting the door.

David stood dumfounded, staring at his wife as she wove her way to their bedroom. She stumbled into their room and turned off the light, leaving the door open as an invitation. But to whom? Rooted in place, David stared at where Liz had been and, gradually, he focused on the framed photograph at the far end of the hallway. It was a wedding picture, but of their assembled party, parents and friends. It was odd...he'd always thought it was a photo of them.

******* ******* *******

Sometimes sleep deprivation will trigger the truth more effectively than threats or violence. Hose them down and make them walk in circles. Place them in a locker and pound it with a stick. Force them to sit on a block of ice while a guard yells at them in a language they can't comprehend.

That night David had trouble sleeping as Liz kept getting up and pacing around their bed. No, it was more like dancing. He could feel her stare at him with her bewitching green eyes, but he tossed and turned, trying to press his eyes shut, afraid to speak, afraid of his wife of twenty-two years.

She was taking off the next day to lead a training in Kansas City. He'd wanted to talk to her for weeks, but she'd become an emotional cauldron: equal parts love and anger, lust and despair, outbursts and obsession. She often could not remember the worst of what she said or did. This had been going on for months now. Life had become so complicated lately. Maybe it had always been that way and he'd only had the illusion of control.

Her dance turned into a waltz, with her following, then leading an armful of air. As his wife dipped and swirled around him, he thought back to his only affair. It had not had much passion and fizzled almost as soon as it had begun. Her name was Harriet and he'd met her toward the end of his stint as a Russian linguist and military in-terrogator. He started the affair following several rounds of after-class drinks during a CIA course they were both taking in DC, before the cold war went stale like an American lager left too long in the sun.

David's first exposure to the capitol was dizzying, filled with secrets, innuendoes, and lust. He made love during lunch hour to Harriet, an N.S.A. agent who made her living opening other people's mail. While lying together she would tell them the secrets she and uncovered, most of it affairs. David had never figured out how to stop people from telling him the truth, except that his own family seemed immune.

Liz spun and flung out her arms by the headboard, her hair lightly brushing the tip of his nose as she now shimmied to a light salsa beat. She was an army brat and they had met when he was still a teenager learning Russian at the Defense Language Institute in Monterey. She had followed him to Germany as the wall fell, living at bases all across the country, and watched him go off to the first Gulf War with two young children left behind. She had convinced him of the darkness that would fall over his profession at Abu Ghraib and other hidden prisons, and he walked away from the only life he had known. Something in him still yearned to break men like bread sticks.

They relocated back to DC, the land of milk, honey, and lucrative government contracts. Liz had studied organizational development at several colleges and she found a job as a trainer at Aries. She had convinced him to apply as a salesman, and they had both worked there for over a decade. Now he was a shining star at Aries while Liz was relegated to training. She had too many morals to thrive as a consultant to executives—she told difficult truths that her clients didn't want to hear.

Liz finally stopped dancing and crawled back into bed, burrowing her head into his chest. Now the tears would start. David held his wife, knowing none of the soothing words that came tumbling to his lips would do any good until she cried herself to sleep. To save his marriage, the former interrogator would need to ask the most import questions of his life. To himself. Who was he beneath his current uniform of suit and tie? And what was he willing to do to save his wife and family?

****** ******* *******

Watch for gaps in their stories. Make them account for their day, then grill them about discrepancies or time shifts. The truthful ones are often angry and shoot accusations back. The ones who evade questions or dispute facts with "There's no case against me," have something to hide.

"What were you two doing yesterday?" David asked, his boys wolfing down cereal at the dining room table at breakneck speed. The two of them had been in cahoots all week with Liz gone, needing a common enemy to stand each other's company.

"Well, Raymond? Don't tell me the movies again.

Leo swallowed the last sip of milk from his glass bowl,

wiped his mouth with a corner of his napkin and said, "Dad, don't take it out on us because Mom's not calling you."

Leo rose calmly and put his bowl into the sink to rinse. "Coming, Raymond?" he asked, walking out the door. His shocked older brother stood with mouth agape and stumbled out after him, no longer the oldest, no longer the one in control.

David picked at his own cereal, picking at what had just transpired. As a boy, Leo had been filled with endless questions: do parakeets have bones? Do actors have bones. Do houseplants and presidents have bones? Do bones have bones? And now the questions his youngest asked him had barbs, much like his own.

David found his interrogator training next to useless when it came to his sons, his wife, anyone he cared about. He'd failed to work up the nerve to talk to Liz before she left. Raymond and Leo could sense his foul mood and were making a career out of making themselves scarce. David was master of his domain in every aspect of his life, confident and respected, except where it counted most— in affairs of the heart. He knew Liz's bizarre behavior was only the tip of the iceberg. He was no less flawed.

******* ******* *******

The body tells realities we've yet to imagine. A truthful subject leans forward in her chair, aggressively, defending her position.

A deceiver slumps far back from you, using the chair or other people around her as a barrier to keep the interrogator away.

"Sorry, Liz, I can barely hear you."

"The bar is pretty loud, I guess."

"At the airport?"

"No, I'm still at my hotel killing time before my flight."

The cellular phone whined from static. David's grip tightened on the receiver as he dodged in and out of traffic.

"I see."

Liz giggled and David overheard at least two different men laughing over the din of voices.

"I have to go, dear. I'm afraid I'm getting myself in trouble again. I told a few of the fellows here how unfair I thought it was that women had to show so much skin in their business attire, so they're unbuttoning their shirts."

"Liz, I have to go, too. Looks like there's an accident further ahead. The traffic's hell."

"What?"

Again the cackling men. David hung up his cell phone and laughed himself, switching lanes, accelerating. He was going to be late for his meeting in Springfield. Again. The Henry G. Shirley Memorial Highway was clogged and it wasn't even rush hour.

He swerved into the carpool lane and passed a few slow-moving cars, dreading seeing his wife later that evening. She'd probably be exhausted from her training and

there would no doubt be another Friday night kegger filling his house with hollow cheer. He spotted a cop on the
shoulder of the road and swerved back out of the faster
carpool lane, cursing the insufficient highway, pushing
the needle of his gas tank gauge below EMPTY. "God
dammit, Liz," he said, slapping his horn. "God dammit!"

******* ******* *******

*If you don't have suitable restraints, use their bootlaces.
More than 95% of POWs will answer all your direct questions.
Torture is unreliable. You can always switch from a good guy
approach to being a hard-ass, but never the other way around.*

"So what's the use teaching the bitch a lesson if she's
not smart enough to get the point?"

"I know what you mean," David said, even though he
didn't. His thoughts kept drifting during his meeting with
Chad Harris. He knew he should get his act together and
pretend to be interested. After all, Hitech Solutions was
his biggest client. Half of being a good consultant was
listening to these assholes' problems.

David stared across the oak table, polished to a manic
gleam, at his client whose fingers twitched as though he
needed a smoke. "So to make a long story short, my wife,
and my girlfriend missed each other by less than five minutes. My life passed in front of my eyes, I swear to God."

"Hmm." David followed the twittering wrist to the neck-

16

line of a now-wrinkled dress shirt. Seeing Chad stare at him expectantly, he asked, "Which one were you scared of most?"

"You kidding? Between those two? It's like choosing between death by drowning or by fire." Chad grinned at his own wit. David could almost see the stitches of last year's hair transplant through the glare of over-bright fluorescents and Grecian formula. "I'm between a rock and a soft place, you might say."

David chuckled and hated what was expected of him. When he'd sold Chad on Aries' services he had used one of his favorite ex-interrogator tricks-of-the-trade. He'd shared a story where he'd embarrassed himself in front of a two-star General. Of course, it was a lie. Chad could relate to it anyway. As product development director, he'd just been reprimanded for a testing glitch on his pet project, Lightning, a new ground-to-air missile system.

"Christ. Answering my car phone's like playing Russian Roulette. They actually expect me to recognize their voices," David said, referring to the imaginary girlfriends he'd created to get in good with Chad.

"Fucking hassle."

David knew that people opened up to you only if you made yourself vulnerable first. And once they did, they were usually so cut off from their emotions that their whole life story came spewing out like blood from a severed artery or a bullet to the heart. He'd used the same technique to score his first date with Liz, charming his way into her bed a few hours after meeting her. She was one of those women who thought they were tough-as-nails, but were really easy marks. That first night he got her to spill her guts about her first sexual experience and stories she swore she'd never shared with anyone before.

He missed her. Terribly. Even when Liz was home, it was obvious that something was changing inside of her. She'd become forgetful, her behavior more and more inexplicable. Her personality was at once breezy and intense, an escalator of emotions. He feared it was the onset of Alzheimer's. He feared she was on drugs. He feared she'd fallen out of love with him. He feared all of the above.

"Hey, it's Bridgette's night over at The Martini Shack." Chad slurred the name of the brunette waitress to make her sound half-French. David was beat, but nodded anyway. He didn't want to go out, but knew this was one of the prices he paid for being a salesman.

"Oui," David said, channeling bad high school French. "Drinks are on me."

******* ******* *******

Silence is one of the most effective tools of interrogation, especially when a subject is pensive and nervous. The fear of what may happen is always greater than what has already come to pass.

He and Liz didn't talk that evening, or about anything more significant the remainder of the weekend than what to eat or what sitcom to watch. David found himself avoiding her over the next few weeks, although he knew her problem wasn't something that could be ignored forever. For a few months he was able to convince himself that he was looking out for her by not bringing it up. The truth was that he was the one frightened—of losing her or that she might never get better.

Leo tiptoed up to him one night in his study after Liz had broken down in tears from watching The Disney Channel. "Dad," his son said simply, "Mom's waiting for you. We're waiting for you."

But David found himself frozen with indecision. Every morning he would attempt to broach the subject with Liz and every day he found some excuse not to. It's kind of cute, he'd tell himself when she sang to the radio that didn't work or forgot his name. Talking to her now was like listening to a favorite record, scratched and filled with crackles and pops, but still infinitely dear.

Who, what, when, where, why, how: the question words, still the best tools for finding out what you need to know. Visualize the scene from the POW's perspective and fill in the holes.

How in God's name was he supposed to live with himself? What if she blamed him for making her a prisoner to a disease with a twelve-syllable name or to drugs that harmed her as much as helped? Before now, the truth always seemed something he could lasso and bring to bay, something that only applied to strangers.

******* ******* *******

It's shocking how many secrets have been uncovered and lives ruined for a single cigarette, a piece of Swiss chocolate, a letter home. Showing you care is the key to any exchange, from business to love to treachery. But never promise more than you can deliver. Some truths even interrogators need to follow.

If someone had peeked into the conference room, just then, it would have had the ambience of a séance with the lights on. Each of Aries' staff meetings started with hands held and a silent prayer. Two dozen trainers and consultants sat in a horseshoe, the backbone of a liberally-bent and yet profitable company. Eyes snapped open and the meeting launched immediately into their yearly marketing strategy. The battlefield had been forming for months, ever since David had scored his deal with Hitech. Some of the assembled group thought that Aries was losing its heart, its mission. David thought too many people in the company were afraid to ruffle feathers or say what they meant.

Their own technology was to blame. Aries' Ten Steps to Employee Empowerment™—which they sold in droves to the stupefied masses—had just the creepiest tinge of breaking down people emotionally and then building them back up. The subtle manipulations in the workshops were familiar to David. There were others who worked here, however, who used empowerment as an adjective and placed absolute faith in the nobility of themselves and others.

Nathan Frost, the founder of Aries, and author of the well-known "Heart, Body, Mind, Workplace Satisfaction" facilitated the heated conversation, controlling what was said like the master manipulator he was. It was no surprise that the person who won the first TV show Survivor was an organizational development professional. They make their living helping people to feel good about owning up to their dark nature, not unlike an interrogator.

"We're working for all the major oil and petrochemical companies," Liz said, "not to mention aerospace. It's just plain wrong."

Nathan paced in front of the room. "And this makes you feel...."

"Like we're only in it for the money."

David fiddled with his tie and burst in with, "Liz, we decided last month not to work for Philip Morris, for God's sake."

"You know that's bullshit, David. The contract was small and that made it a hell of a lot easier for us to be righteous."

"Don't you think these companies deserve to have empowered employees, too?"

"Why, so they can rape the environment more efficiently?"

David didn't even try and hold it back. He glared at Liz with all the frustration he'd been storing up.

"Fuck you, too!" Liz said, bolting out of her seat. She bumped several swivel chairs and barged out of the conference center into the main office. David rose, apologized to the room, and followed his wife's trail. He dashed past the receptionist and tracked her into one of the private meeting rooms where she sat, bawling into her fists.

He kneeled and wrapped his arms around her. "It's OK."

But it was anything but OK. He couldn't help but wondering what was driving his wife to the brink: menopause, brain cyst, meth-amphetamines?

"Don't you think we should be able to have some fucking control over the work we do?"

"Shhh," he said as she bucked in his embrace.

"Just a little fucking control, is that too much to ask?"

For this he had no answer.

******* ******* *******

A foxtrot on a packed dance floor—that's what interrogation seems most like sometimes. Intimacy is the key to good dancing and unguarded conversation. Kindness are the hands, anger the feet, questions the rhythm, while the music crescendos in the interrogator's hands, who has left thought behind and can use the resistance of his partner to propel them to where he needs to go.

Dinner that night with his parents at Maury's Grill was a subtle brand of torture. His folks had moved to town last year after early retirement to "be close to him," although they'd never been close before. Liz was distracted and quiet, picking at her food. Both of his sons had managed to duck out of the engagement.

"Two months. It's been two months since I've seen my grandsons."

"They had plans, Dad. Raymond's out with his friends and Leo's got dress rehearsal for a play he's in."

"Another play?"

"Yes, Mom, he's got the lead this time."

His father snorted. "I can't believe my Leo isn't here because he wants to practice being a puffter."

"What did you say?"

"You heard me, son, a puffter."

Several heads turned from the booth next to them. Liz smiled, but her words were pure venom, "Look, Felix, Leo is applying himself to something, unlike Raymond who is out carousing with his buddies. How come you never say anything bad about him?"

"Liz, if you don't want my opinion just say so, the last thing I would ever do is intrude on how you raise your sons."

"All right then, shut the fuck up. You too, Ruth. I know what you're thinking."

"David, are you going to let her talk to your mother like that? I didn't say anything."

"Come on, let's all be reasonable, Mom, Liz."

"Once a month we ask them to dinner. How could we be any less obtrusive?"

"Dad, I know...look-"

Liz rose. "Quiet, this is my song."

"What is she talking about, David, I don't hear any song."

Liz fluttered gracefully to a small opening between tables. It didn't take long for the packed restaurant to take notice with her swaying between tables, pirouetting to waiters, using tables and chairs as impromptu partners.

There are some dark corners where even the most skilled dancers cannot navigate.

"David, what in God's name is she doing?"

"She's dancing. She needs a partner," he explained.

Fear is one reason. Unwilling to lose control another. Denial. Hatred. Love.

"I'm going to talk to her, Mom."

Liz started singing, loudly, "Is there nothing I can say, nothing I can do? To change your mind, I'm so in love with you. I wanna be your emotional rescue."

Oh no, not this. Couldn't she sing a nice show tune instead of disco-era Rolling Stones?

"Bu bomp, bu bomp, be bomp bomp buh." David

reached Liz's side and grabbed her hand. "Bu bomp, bu bomp, bu bomp bomp buh."

The true professional never stops learning new steps to cajole, dazzle and invigorate — the perfect spin, swivel or dip into meaning.

She whirled as though they'd rehearsed a dance number and he followed her lead. He felt his own voice go falsetto, "Yeah, baby I'm crying...over you...."

Here's the real secret of interrogation—to be more lost than anyone in the music. The interrogator holds his partner close in the lights and tries not to let go.

They continued dancing and singing and butchering lyrics while the crowd clapped and his parents grimaced. Finally, when they had repeated the same refrain for the third time, David dipped her and held her close. He thought about what questions it would take to reach her: *Who are we, what are we, when are we, why are we, how are we...*

She held him tightly and he whispered, "I'm sorry. We can't go on like this can we?"

"No." He pulled her back to her feet and lifted the veil of hair from her eyes.

"I'm scared."

"Me, too."

They might be fine as a couple or might not. Their sons might be scarred by this or would use family strife to make themselves stronger. Liz might need to be medicated by something that would poison her even as it cured her. Truth would set the interrogator inside of him free so that the man hidden there could emerge. David kissed his wife's brow and held her hand as the world spun around them dizzily. He would not let them fall.

Virgin of the Parkway

Bianca had lived through many things in her 73 years—one war, one daughter, one grandson, one death that would never be discussed in her house, one move from New York to Seattle, an area shrouded as much in mist as the impenetrable customs of youth. There was much in life she still didn't understand, but she had to admit at least things were lively in her daughter's new home. Her neighbors—mostly young Mexican families, elderly Italian immigrants, and working class whites—were filled with stories about their patch of city below the freeway overpass: a fire at the paint factory that grayed the sky for three nights and two days, a fatal police shooting of two 13-year-old boys who'd gone on a joy ride in a stolen car, and a three million dollar lottery winner from New York who'd bought the ticket at their corner store. Her neighbors saw these events as omens, signs that nothing good would ever happen to them or their neglected warehouse district.

But none of them had seen anything quite like The Virgin of the Parkway.

The statue appeared mysteriously one morning on the hilltop of a small park overlooking the freeway feeding into the city from the Eastern suburbs. The Virgin was a mishmash of used appliances, trash bin treasures, and household junk. Her head had been hammered out of an aluminum teakettle. Her eyes were copper pennies painted cerulean, peering out at a stream of traffic. Her pelvis was an ancient computer screen, mannequin arms crossed over the birdcage that served as her chest. She wore red carpeting cut like a shawl. Twin candleholders—which held curtain rods—were her feet, and all of it was soldered in bronze and painted a flesh tone that blushed in the sun.

Bianca was not altogether surprised when her daughter Isabella started joining the stream of Catholics leaving flowers and candles at the foot of the Parkway "miracle." It was Clara, Isabella's best friend, who'd first seen the resemblance to the holy mother. Clara was Mexican and shared the same religious fervor of Italian Catholics, a belief that was equal measure fear and hope, guilt and redemption.

Bianca's own beliefs had been shaken by her litany of losses. She had spent too many years waiting for a heavenly hand to reach down and lift the curse from her family, or at least give her a sign that one day it might happen. And Bianca had lost much in the process of waiting. She viewed the world suspiciously. Her daughter's friends were jackals. She no longer had control of her hands, which shook in both the heat and cold. And instead of looking skyward, she kept her eyes down to the garbage, to the earth. Signs were formed by people, not God.

The more Bianca pushed away religion, the more Isabella clung to the notion. It put them at odds over almost every household decision. The tension had been escalating for years now, unspoken, a powder keg. After all she'd been through it was too much for Bianca to put the fate of her family in God's hands. And yet her survival in her daughter's home depended on biting her lip and clamping her mouth and shutting herself in her room when things exploded between her daughter and Mauro, her grandson, who was 14 going on 40.

She loved them both, but they needed her guidance, even if they didn't have sense enough to know it. So here she was, relegated to eavesdropping on her family as she had earlier that evening when she sat in bed reading a recipe book she had long ago memorized.

"Mama, it's none of your business where I am, not after school and not at night when you're out with your creepy friends," Mauro said.

It had taken every bit of self-control not to rush out in the living room and scream at them both. Generally, Mauro had more sense than her daughter, but like everyone in the family, he had an impetuous streak when backed into a corner.

"Stay out of my business."

"You are my business, Mauro."

"You're doing a great job of taking care of me, just like you did Dad."

There was a heavy silence. Bianca slid off the bed and tiptoed to the door.

"We all make decisions, Mauro, and it looks like you just made yours. You're grounded."

"Until when?"

"Until I say you're not grounded."

"I wish you were the one who died."

Bianca'd had enough. Consequences be damned, she went out into the living room to find the two people she loved most staring each other down. Although she knew sage advice from the old country was what was called for, all she could manage was, "I can make dinner tonight."

Isabella and Mauro turned their backs and two doors were slammed by two people who shared such a deep hurt they could no longer live in the same house without hurting each other. Bianca's own worries, like many Italian mothers' and grandmothers', were turned inward. Only there were no men left to lay down the law of the house with baritones and breath made sweet and sour with wine. So instead, Bianca looked to eradicate the cobwebs of her home and memories. She cleaned neurotically, read insatiably.

Now here it was ten after nine on a Thursday night, just hours after the fight, and she was left alone to contemplate the future. Both Isabella and Mauro had stomped out and if past experiences were any indication, neither would be home for hours, a double dare with no one to collect the bets but Bianca. And, of course, they never considered her failing health, Mauro's schoolwork, or her daughter's inevitable bleary-eyed race out the door the next morning to her job as a paralegal downtown.

So it was up to her to model responsibility for her family, even if they weren't around to notice. She'd already exorcised the house of all dust and was now left fretting about the small nooks of clutter that encircled their living room like drunken spectators at a bullfight. Mexican jar candles—presents from Clara—cluttered the windowsills and end tables. All were half-filled, the wicks drowning in wax from candle-lit dinners past. Photographs of missing men dominated the mantelpiece. Bianca's long-departed husband, Isabella's Kurt, and their own Mauro, lost in spirit if not in body.

The houseplants bothered her most of all. Isabella had "rescued" them from the office, and brought them to the house to die. A half dozen scrawny rhododendrons and spider plants, surrounded by a ring of brown and yellow leaves, were given a strange place of honor, one in each room. Mauro ignored them as best he could and Bianca could not bring herself to water them.

No matter where she turned she could not escape the signs of misfortune: buried wicks, missing men, dying plants. It was as though she could feel the world close around her, suffocating her, burying her...and her family with it. Earlier that afternoon she had picked up the phone in the kitchen only to hear Mauro on the other line bragging to his friends about how he had the balls to join their gang and that he would show them tonight what he was made of.

Bianca waited for the front door to close, accompanied by Mauro's still-boyish scamper down the front steps, then called her daughter at work. She got no further than the words "Mauro" and "gang," when Isabella hung up on her, swearing in bastard Italian that would have made her Dom roll in his grave.

Bianca could no longer carry the burden of her worry for her grandson. She put on her coat and headed outside, shocked at how slick and cool the winter had become. The older she got the more time seemed to accelerate, days melting into days past, neighbors blending slowly into the visage of childhood friends and old phobias returning: fear of the dark, fear of spiders, fear of being alone.

Three houses down, she saw a light on in Clara's house. Her steps on the sidewalk were small and insignificant, like her body. Her fear of a tumble on ice and a broken hip took away any joy she might have in a stroll. She paused outside her neighbor's door long enough to hear the laughter of women's voices before knocking. Clara answered, a downpour of giggles coming from the living room. The smile on her lips was as mischievous as a child's.

"Oh, this is unexpected. Please come in. Bella, your mother's here."

Bianca shed her jacket and said hello to Clara's sister Rosaria and Yolanda—the corner storeowner's wife—before sitting next to her daughter on the couch. A glass pitcher of sangria was on the coffee table next to a plate of chips and salsa. Skeletons from Mexican folk art watched the small gathering from surrounding tables and ledges, alongside lit jar candles and ceramic figurines of jungle animals.

"Can I get you anything?"

"No, Clara, nothing for me."

Isabella slid her wine glass behind a vase, but her cheeks were rosy from more than the heat of the fire, her voice fearless and lubricated. "Mother, we were just talking about the Virgin and how it hasn't rained since she showed up on the Parkway."

"Mildest winter in decades," Clara said, pouring herself

another glass of sangria. "And Yolanda's cat Molo came back after being away for more than two years."

"And Rosaria's boyfriend just asked her to marry him," Yolanda said, laughing. "And you only have to have met Luis once to know there must be some divine intervention for that to happen."

Rosaria pinched her friend on the forearm and hissed, "Jealous."

"I'm still waiting," Clara said. "I've left flowers at the statue every day, but no Prince Charming for me. Yet."

"Mama doesn't approve," Isabella said. "She doesn't believe in miracles, not since World War II."

Bianca felt suddenly embarrassed, wondering if Isabella had told them of her endless reminiscence about the war and her long journey alone to New York, a daughter in her belly and no money in her pockets.

"I need to talk to you, Isabella."

"So talk, Mom, we're all friends here."

"Mauro hasn't come home yet and—"

"He's throwing a tantrum."

"And what are you doing, Isabella? Filled with the holy spirit, I take it?"

"Yes, I am. I'll be vindicated in the next life, Mama."

"But what about this life? What about Mauro? What about the danger I tried to warn you about?"

Isabella glared at her mother with twin brown scythes.

"How about a glass, Bianca," Clara said, trying to ease the tension. "You must be freezing." She reached over the table to pour a glass, nearly spilling the pitcher.

Bianca considered the offer: the allure of drinking herself into oblivion on a night her grandson needed her, the tackiness of swilling a festive summer drink on a cold winter night. It would be so easy to try to forget the past...and the future, but just one look at her daughter's drunken glare made up her mind for her. "No thank you, Clara," she said. "I'm going out to find my grandson. Good night, ladies."

Bianca rose and buttoned her coat, matching her daughter's disapproval eye for eye. The mood in the room had chilled; voices and glasses stopped mid-motion. Bianca stared at the small ring of sangria under the pitcher's base, feeling much like the red sweet wine seeping into scratched wood. She turned and moved to the door, almost stopping to tell Isabella how, late that afternoon, she had spied on Mauro and his friends hanging out at the corner store, scrounging for someone to score them a bottle.

"Mama, I'll walk you home." Isabella called out behind her.

"No need," Bianca said. "I'll manage." She stepped outside into the crisp night air. "I always do."

She paused on the porch to catch her breath, suddenly tired. If she closed her eyes she could almost imagine the traffic sounds from the parkway were the crashing waves of the Mediterranean from her childhood in Sicily. She should never have left her Dom to run off to her cousins in New York during the first rumblings of war. But how could she have known she'd never see him again?

Bianca opened her eyes and noticed a glimmer on the hilltop of the parkway clearing, the Virgin glowing oddly in the cascade of headlights. She wasn't sure exactly what drew her up the grassy incline toward the statue. The park was the last place a woman her age should be at night. Perhaps she felt a need to see Mary with all her flaws and tragic beauty, to remember what she had been like when she was young. Or could it be that deep down she still believed in God, if not a merciful one, then one who occasionally visited the gloom of Seattle? There were many types of signs, she reminded herself. Burning bushes, swastikas, statues rising, people disappearing in the night.

As she climbed, Bianca could see the matronly silhouette set against the freeway high beams and overcast night shroud, a ghostly reminder of the Virgin from her hometown church, long destroyed by war. She felt a sharp chill burrow into her skin and a pang in her hips. She stopped in her tracks, lost, a woman without a home.

Then her resolve returned. One small step led to another. As she moved closer to the Virgin, she could see shadows and hear men's voices, then finally orange and red candles tossing light on bare trees and yellow grass. And a boy lying face down in the flowers at the foot of the Virgin. She recognized the jacket.

"Jesus Christ, there's someone coming up the path."

"Puta madre, it's just some old bat. This is a private party."

The two shadows turned to teenage boys from the neighborhood: one white, the other Latino, both reeking of liquor and cigarette smoke. Bianca ignored the scowls and flickering freeway lights, rushing to where Mauro lay unconscious, face down on a blanket of rose petals and lilies. Please, please, please let him be all right. If anyone was supposed to die, it was her. She gently turned her grandson onto his back and placed an ear over his mouth to see if he was breathing.

A rough hand grabbed her by the shoulder. "Are you deaf, old lady?"

Bianca made the sign of the cross, her fierce look sending the boy accosting her backwards several steps.

"You should be ashamed of yourselves. You're supposed to be Mauro's friends. What did he drink?"

"Beer and tequila."

"The whole pint."

Bianca gripped Mauro's jacket and pulled his head forward, sticking a finger down his throat. The vomit was instantaneous, followed by coughing and the whoops and laughs of the boys as they raced down the incline toward their own oblivious families.

Mauro crawled to his hands and knees and spit out the contents of his stomach. First dinner, then tequila, then air as he heaved and heaved. Finally, Bianca helped him to his feet and gave him a shoulder to lean on as they stumbled down the path.

"I'm sorry, Grandma, first time I drank. First time."

"Do you realize you could have killed yourself?" Rage replaced fear in Bianca's voice. "Do you?"

Mauro dipped his head and bawled into the sleeve of his jacket. The last time she'd seen him cry was the day his father died. Her son-in-law Kurt had been depressed for weeks toward the end of his unemployment as a city engineer and had fought with Isabella all weekend. While the family sat and watched TV, Kurt slipped outside to water the plants on the tiny deck overlooking the Chelsea alley. The police had their suspicions about what happened next and so did the insurance company, which fought paying off the life policy, but one thing was clear. Kurt had not made a sound on his way down. Mauro went outside to check on his father and had found the hose leading from the sink spilling out over the balcony, his father eleven stories below.

Accidents happen. Death happened. People fell, but sometimes they rose again. Although her hip was flaring from arthritis, Bianca kept her grandson moving forward. When they finally reached home, Mauro stumbled immediately into his mother's arms, who had taken the anger of an old lady to heart and had raced home. Mother and son stood like statues as Bianca marched to the hall closet where she fished out the baseball bat they kept for family protection. There was unfinished business she needed to attend to—she would no longer live at the mercy of the signs surrounding her.

Bianca strode out the door, a ridiculous-looking figure she was sure. Isabella and Mauro did not notice her, nor did she want them to. Some things were better left a mystery.

****** ******* ******

When Bianca returned later that evening she found her daughter and grandson asleep on the couch, his head resting on her shoulder. She took off her coat, tossed the bat in the back of the closet, and went to her room where she managed to get the best night's sleep she'd had in years. Imagine, falling asleep again before midnight. A miracle.

When she woke, it was raining outside, the beginning of one of those impressive three-week Seattle storms. Isabella and Mauro were having breakfast, both playing hooky, already buzzing with the latest neighborhood gossip. Earlier that morning the Virgin of the Parkway had disappeared as mysteriously as it had arrived. There were no signs of departure, leaving the neighborhood with portents and omens they would not remember past spring.

Life continued on in the Parkway even without the Virgin overseeing their lives. Clara did not find her Prince Charming. Her sister Rosaria was heartbroken by Luis who ran off with Yolanda, the corner storeowner's wife, although she did adopt Yolanda's tomcat Molo, now her constant companion. And Bianca actually began going to church again. Perhaps it was the influence of the Virgin Mary, planted in the back yard beneath a new bed of spring begonias and lilies. Somehow in the giddiness of clear spring days, her family and neighbors had not noticed her moving the statue she had hidden behind the corner store dumpster piece by piece to her garden. Religion like love thrived best when close at hand, pressed to the heart.

And as for her own family? The conflict between mother and son intensified for a time. Isabella and Mauro kept fighting, but stopped running out on each other, stopped trying to follow Kurt off the edge of the earth. They complained about the other's bad habits and, eventually, like an old couple in their twilight years, stopped doing the tiny things that pissed the other off.

Bianca started hanging out in the living room at night with her family as her grandson did homework and her daughter cleaned up after dinner. She started speaking her mind and, although her advice was rarely appreciated, Bianca preferred sighs and rolling eyes to the purgatory of her bedroom. Some nights Bella's friends came over, sometimes his. Mother and son both dated, but never at the same time. And they all took turns watering the plants, which began to thrive in the glow of company, conversation, and lit candles. It became a messy house, a cluttered house, home.

Intersection

The trouble began during the winter rainy season when we were trying to decide whether to make love standing at a busy intersection, specifically the corner of Noe and Market Street several blocks from our home. Like most married couples we've had our share of fantasies and tribulations. In the past, we acted on our desires: leaving the shades open and lights on while we had sex, making dates with each other at a bar and pretending we'd just met, driving to the Marin Headlands and making love in World War II bunkers. But we let this traffic fantasy eat at us until we were frustrated that we could not get what we wanted.

Spring didn't bring us any relief from the damp San Francisco cold and the mildew that lingered in our home. I kept waking up at odd hours in our drafty apartment and discovering that Victoria had stolen the covers from me. To make things worse, she kept forgetting to turn off the alarm. The blare of classic rock radio woke us at six on Sunday. She grumbled and swatted at the snooze. I scrambled over her cool torso and pulled out the plug, digging my elbow into her breast for leverage.

"Hey," she said.

"Hey," I repeated, noticing minute red scratches on the inside of her left thigh that could have been from anything.

She looked amused at my confusion and said, "Just irritation from sliding into home plate," although she had never shown any interest in sports before.

For some reason, our worst arguments began in the mornings. We both hated putting on the coffee pot.

"I made it last time," she said.

"I wash the dishes and take out the trash."

"I make more money than you and work more hours."

I work in direct mail, catalogues, an antiquated profession responsible for three percent of deforestation (a statistic Victoria often quotes, particularly at parties). She's a landscaper for Pacific Heights lawyers, doctors, and politicians. It wasn't until recently that we'd begun noticing the differences between us.

"*All* the dishes and *all* the trash," I said, rolling over onto my side. Angry teeth chewed the insides of my cheek. "Home plate should be at home," I finally spat out.

It had come to this: baseball analogies. One moment we were enjoying sex several times a week, then the next, kaput. Neither of us could let go of the desire to roll with the other beneath the squeal of automobiles. Last week we even tried to make out with open raincoats on the intersection traffic island, neither of us wearing underwear, but we lost our nerve. We'd actually begun to spend less time with each other because of it, taking separate walks in the hills above our home, going to different bars, finding ticket stubs to Giants games.

Pangs of jealousy had slowly devoured the sheets off our bed until we could only keep warm with tattered promises. She'd stripped the blankets from our double mattress because of the poison that seeped from the scratches on her thigh like a cigarette discarded in a bed of parched field grass.

I thought about therapy for the both of us—her imaginary poison, my fear of imaginary lovers. Twin impotence from a desire to have our love seen for the horrible shuddering thing it was. Sometimes I scratched her legs while she slept, particularly after she drank heavily. Silence leapt between our lips in wind-swept leaves of fire, like dried-out insurance policies ringing the Oakland Hills in summer. First her thigh, then my hand swelled with uncontrollable urges. Soon Market Street was one gigantic rash of shuddering steel and whining glass.

I did not stop sinking my fingernails into her flesh until all the world scratched each other's thighs—billions of fingernails sinking through green meat, clawing at the cracked and bone-red sunset. It made me feel better to realize that others' jealousy ran much deeper than my own.

"Why do they line the infield baselines with gravel instead of dirt?" she asked when she woke.

I said, "Because the world needs lovers to have skinned knees."

I stared down at the hardwood floor and noticed my boots, caked with chalk, beneath a pile of clothing. She told me that she was jealous of my afternoon walks. Our fears molded, reversed. My hands and legs burned with the itch of desire. Poison.

"It seems unfair when catchers block home plate," she said.

"Collisions are part of the game," I teased.

Faintly, the horns of passing traffic and brakes squeaked through the cracked window. I felt something poke me from under the mattress and reached under the edge of the futon. I pulled out a rusted lug wrench and held it up to the morning light streaming through the blinds. I couldn't remember if I had placed it there for prowlers or if we'd ever needed it to change a tire.

I raised my eyebrows. She began laughing. "You never know," she said.

"No, you never do." I pulled her close and tried to ignore the grass stains on the bedding, but not the itching. The terrible whine of skin.

"Coffee?" she asked.

"Yeah, I'll make it."

Bulldog

Kay's Ford Dealership on Sawdust Road was known for the face—not of the owner on the signage outside the refurbished tin warehouse—but of the bulldog Maurie, who patrolled the shining deals-of-the-week and repossessed wrecks with a limp, the onset of cataracts, and a bilious wheeze. At least, that's what Junior Kay thought, looking at life through the lens of a hockey mask and the belief that he was responsible for deflecting all bad things from entering his area of control. Stopping the pucks of opposing hockey players from bouncing into his net. Keeping his dad from getting too drunk on work nights. Blocking thoughts of his departed mother from entering his mind or, worse, his father's.

J.K. even felt protective of his hometown. Twelve Point made up the index finger tip of Michigan's lower peninsula and had the kind of character you'd find in a favorite uncle who looked like a serial killer, but was ultimately soft-hearted. The grumpy gulls on the Lake Huron shores brayed at tourists for breadcrumbs. Fresh trout hooked from the bay carried a chemical cocktail in their flesh as they were smothered in beer batter and deep fried. Polkas and jigs at wedding receptions at the VFW Hall involved the shaking of doughy flesh and at least one person falling over a chair, child, or dog. And there was, of course, an undying devotion to the American automobile—the subject of many of his dad's rants.

That's why townsfolk paid attention on the January day when the sleek Japanese sedan came roaring in from the south past Kay's Ford, gray snow spewing in its wake. Its windows were tinted and there was no trust in that. In Twelve Point, the driver's seat and the lazy-boy were the chairs closest to God. Only men with dark thoughts hid behind the wheel of a foreign car or, at least, that's what Kay Senior proposed to the gang over at the Elks' Lodge the weekend before, while J.K. watched his beloved Red Wings on the big-screen TV.

Twelve Point wasn't noted for its subtleties. A stuffed 12-point deer posed proudly in a glass case on U.S. 23 North within view of Lake Huron's stony shores. The 3-year-old trophy buck gazed at passersby with glazed eyes from the horror it had faced one winter morning decades ago as it stared down the sights of a 30-30 Python while munching the half-sour field apples trucked in as bait.

The Walleye River sliced the town in two, a dividing line for the original German and Polish settlers, who still waged battles decades past when anyone could explain why the hostility should continue. Perhaps it was the well-kept houses shellacked with aluminum siding on the German south side, and the dump on the north slopes that made any wind from Canada fill the Polish half with a stench that drove the residents to the factories to escape it. Perhaps it was something hidden.

As the Japanese car cut through the heart of town, it wasn't long before everyone knew who drove it—Dyson Dietrich. The old German had returned to settle his score with Kay, who'd "changed his name from Kowalski to Kay so he wouldn't sound like a Polack." Or so Dietrich ranted as he settled back in his favorite stool at the Owl Saloon after a fifteen-year absence, waiting for him and Kay to lock horns like rutting elks long after snow had fallen and all the females were already spoken for. At least, this is what the mailman told J.K. and he didn't have any reason not to believe him. So on the night his dad suggested that they head on over to the Owl Saloon for dinner, J.K. pretended that there was nothing out of the ordinary.

******* ******* *******

Junior Kay stood and watched his dad taking a piss on the wheel well of the stranger's car in the bar parking lot, the stream of urine causing steam to rise from the bumper even as the smell joined a foul gust rolling in from the north. J.K. was only sixteen, but had become accustomed to grown men peeing on everything from tree stumps to bathroom floors to themselves. There was something unnerving about the drizzle that caused his imagination to shimmy from the snow-crusted lot, drifting out across the 45th parallel that divided the town as surely as it did the northern hemisphere.

On the north side of Twelve Point, he was certain that Tracy was slipping off her cheerleading uniform, damp from practice, even as she danced in the dark to her favorite radio station, eyes half closed. She would fondle the her pink cell phone, wondering if she should call him or put on her clothes. North. South. Day. Night. All of this melted away. And then there was the sound of a zipper.

His father grunted and kicked the new-fallen white carpeting onto the Japanese sedan for good measure. J.K. thought about mentioning what he'd heard from the postman, but decided better of it as they strode into the Owl.

In the entrance of the pockmarked downtown bar, his Dad showed every crease and worry line of forty-five winters beneath the wool cap that advertised his dealership in gold trim. Behind an oak bar, Eva whistled once, mimicking the gale outside, and Kay shouldered the door closed.

J.K caught sight of a knotty old German across the bar who lifted a glass of draft beer at their entrance, then spit in it, and turned his back.

"Dietrich," his dad hissed, and J.K reacted immediately, making tracks for his Dad's enemy, but Kay held him back. His dad edged in front of him and nodded to Eva, taking off his cap and showing the patience of a man used to talking about salt rust on the underside of chassis for hours at a stretch or sitting motionless in a camouflaged deer blind. Junior Kay felt the bulldog tenacity within him rise. He felt a deep desire to keep his father from getting hurt, from leaving him like his mother did.

J.K carried his tenacity in a scowl that creased his forehead beneath frosted blond hair, but Eva winked at him mischievously instead of being afraid. He'd been told that he had his mother's temper and good looks—there was nothing bulldog-like about the appearance of Twelve Point High's star hockey goalie, no matter the fierce loyalty underneath. J.K. kept close watch on his dad, who eased in next to Dietrich like a piston across from its twin in an old rust bucket's sputtering engine. That's the way their conversation sounded as they coughed out words beneath their graying hoods, the bar silent from the eavesdropping.

J.K. had heard his mother defend Dietrich for years as his dad grumbled about his departed pal turned nemesis. They had all been friends at one time, a closeness that now allowed Kay to lean over and whisper in Dietrich's ear.

It was awkward to watch the two men joined at the face in an almost strange embrace as his father blew air into Dietrich's ear valve and the German burned red in the face. J.K. looked away through the darkened glass at an empty downtown street caked in ice, the sidewalks wearing a train of dark slush from factory stacks. The bar was full on a Friday, with no one but him under thirty. The men were seated elbow to elbow around the TVs. A few old maids played Euchre in the corner and drank from a plastic pitcher. The only one with clear eyes in the entire dive was Eva, his father's age, who stared at them with interest. J.K. tapped his feet and cleared his throat impatiently, until the long whisper came to an end.

Kay pushed himself away from Dietrich until they were in swinging distance. Junior could see that what his father said had gotten to the German, barbs sunk into that leathery red skin. But Dietrich didn't say a word, just returned his spit-in draft to Eva, and swallowed down a neat shot of cinnamon Schnapps.

Dietrich coughed from the slow burn that came over him and smiled, saying, "I'll come to the dealership on Monday and pick up Maurie. It's about time he had a ride in a Japanese car."

Kay shook his head. "I expected more from you, Dee."

"Dad, what's he taking about? There's no way he's getting his hands on Maurie."

J.K. stepped up to Dietrich and took in his Dad's long-time foe, the way he would stare down a rushing winger who'd gotten too close to his net. He glared at the man with his middle-aged paunch, lips chapped from the cold, and flabby cheeks flushed from alcohol. Green eyes set in wide cheekbones bored into him longingly, desperately. J.K.'s fists unclenched and he lost his nerve in that strange, lonely stare.

Snorting for the crowd, J.K. hurried to catch up to his dad, who bowed respectfully to Eva and donned his Kay cap on the way out the door.

******* ******* *******

When J.K. woke Saturday morning, his legs still ached from taking a puck in the knee from where the pads didn't cover during their 3-3 tie with the Alpena Wildcats.

That was the thing about protective gear, seatbelts, chain-link fences—there was always some vulnerable spot. That's why they counted on Maurie to keep his dad's dealership safe—his future business if his hockey career stalled, as it did for most kids up north once they made it to college and realized they were too clumsy, too small, too slow. He'd seen former Twelve Point hockey heroes slinking around town sporting tires around their bellies and working at the paper mill or cement plant.

J.K. rolled off his still-made bed, where he'd passed out listening to the wind beating the tree with ice outside his window. He still wore his jeans and jersey from the after-game bash at Mike's.

Barefoot and limping, he padded out to the kitchen and made himself cereal, hearing his dad spraying down their old Ford pickup in the drive. Something was wrong—after caring for cars all week, Kay never bothered to wash their own, especially not in winter.

J.K. took his bowl of Life out into the driveway, and walked barefoot over the slick cement. He sat on the stoop, watching his father attack the crusted dirt on their truck with a disintegrating sponge and the lawn hose. He and his dad were a lot alike. Since his mom died, they ate meals in the driveway, garage, on the roof, in cars driving home from fast food restaurants, in their beds, in front of the TV, everywhere but at the dining room table she'd once splendidly set. It was now a repository for fishing tackle, snow chains, and ski boots.

After he finished drinking milk from the bottom of the blue flowered bowl his mom had adored, J.K. traced the pattern along it with a spoon in a sweeping figure eight, like when she showed him how to skate. His hand kept moving the aluminum oval along the porcelain roses, recalling her face that had watched over them with creases of worry and a ceaseless vigilance, even at the end when the pain was too much to look her in the eyes.

A few droplets sprayed his hair and he looked up. His dad turned off the water and wiped sweat from his face. "C'mon, boy," he said, "we're hunting today."

******* ******* *******

Maurie rustled behind the bucket seat of the pick-up, sticking his nose out the back window and sucking in air next to the gun rack. It had been nearly five years since J.K. had gone hunting with his dad, but he knew better than to ask why the sudden change. He'd wrapped up his swollen knee, and it took almost an hour to oil their guns, and pack up equipment and the hoagies Aunt Karen had made. They dressed in orange vests that reminded him of the lifejackets stowed on their pontoon named "Heavenly Lisa" for his mom.

In the sky, factory smoke joined winter clouds in a curtain over the town, like the unwashed ones in their living room. They accelerated across the tracks into the Polish corridor and pulled into a gravel field skirting a long bank of apartment buildings, with fading white paint turning the color of slush.

J.K. sat quietly as his dad pounded his fist twice on

the horn. Maurie brayed lightly, not in alarm, but in the confusion that J.K. himself felt. Across the parking field, a man in a faded orange vest ambled up to the truck and Kay leaned on the horn once more.

"Hurry up, you old bastard," Kay said.

Behind him, J.K. heard a low growl in Maurie's throat match the anger in his own chest. Dietrich opened the door and settled in beside him, squashing him into the gear shift that drove into his ribs as his father slapped the truck in gear and spun up ice, road salt, and gravel.

The excited pants and whimpers of Maurie sliding on the floorboard behind them muffled the AM station that Dietrich switched on the stereo. Even through the down of his parka, J.K. could feel the heat emanating from the old man squashed beside him. A country song moaned with static, and Maurie danced along the backboard. Kay drove like he was a young buck, fishtailing his truck through intersections and speeding toward the Huron National Forest.

J.K. felt trapped against the fat German who looked at him hungrily like he was a fast-food drive-through kiosk. Something his mom once said about Dietrich being family burned in the back of his head. J.K. shuddered and thought back instead to last night's bash. They had piled into David Kroft's van as he and his pal took their party-on-wheels over to pick up the rest of the team's defensemen. Then it was a quick trip across the river to pick up Tracy, whose husky voice had already been lost to cheers, cigarettes, and Schnapps the cheerleaders shared under the bleachers.

She had scrunched in front between David and him as they drank from a paper bag and blasted tunes, and rolled out onto Casper Road to find Mike's hunting lodge, where a keg awaited them.

J.K. and David both liked Tracy; it was an unspoken secret. All three of them knew it, and each worked to keep the tension knife-sharp, lying about the others they dated or made out with at parties. Tracy's voice was a deep whisper last night, almost man-like, giving them directions, just as Dietrich did as he led them onto a dirt path off the country road, toward his family's old blind on Huckleberry Ridge. They snaked along the half-logged woods as a wan sun beamed an overcast gray through the remaining stands of trees.

******* ******* *******

Late afternoon loomed beneath the oak lean-to and olive tarp, the frayed ends shimmying in a wind rising up from the lake. From the looks of the clouds, a storm was imminent on the horizon. Black pillows swirled with gray above them. J.K. shivered from the still-drying sweat in his winter jacket, residue from the manic energy that had launched him and Maurie out in the woods to play—anything to keep them away from the two old men fondling rifle grips and passing Southern Comfort between them. The two former friends stared across an open field broken by blackberry bushes and a scruffy hill that kept their heads at the hoof level of any deer breaking through the thicket of pines and underbrush.

"I was in the desert two weeks ago," Dietrich said.

"Should've retired there and saved us all this head-ache," his dad replied, handing back the bottle.

Dietrich unzipped his glove and poured a few fingers of whiskey into two plastic cups—one he handed to J.K. and the other he placed in front of Maurie, whose tired eyes moved from the open field to his doggie treat.

"There are plants with needles you can't see that pierce right into you." Dietrich capped the bottle and slipped on his glove, pulling the rifle barrel into his chest.

"Too bad the needle didn't go straight to your heart." Dad laughed at his own joke, even though J.K. couldn't see what was funny about it.

"Who says it didn't. There's nothing in here but tat-ters." Dietrich thumped his chest with the rifle butt and coughed, his bloodshot eyes the same color as his skin, chapped from his recent immersion in northern elements. "I'm still coming for Maurie tomorrow at noon. Have him at the dealership."

"Over my dead body," J.K. muttered.

Maurie began lapping away at his cup as J.K did the same. This was the dinner that had been handed to them, it seemed. In this strange twilight coming down into both of their lives, he felt as close to Maurie as a brother, lying side by side on an Army blanket thrown across the ground, as silence and nightfall settled over the deer blind.

******* ******* *******

J.K. and David sat in the front seat of the van in the gravel lot outside the fenced-off Ford Dealership. They had skipped P.E.—their teacher was a former All-State winger who didn't care if the jocks slid out of class, focusing his stern attention on the too-skinny geeks with paper-thin wrists.

Between them, in the front of the van, was Tracy's pack of Parliaments. Despite being there to look after Maurie, their eyes kept being drawn down to the light blue-and-white cardboard box, as though it were her costume of the same color as she tossed her leg high in the air at the end of a cheer.

"I know you whisper to Tracy at parties so she'll lean into you," David said, his bitten fingernails digging into the vinyl of the steering column.

"Just being polite. Her voice was shot," J.K. countered. "How about her taking your arm to get to the lodge?"

"It was icy," David said and a coldness hovered momentarily between them.

Outside—through windows fogging over with the condensation of their breathing—J.K. noticed that the lot had begun to fill, as though news of this impending confrontation had already traveled from the north to the south with an ill wind of its own.

As noon approached, the dealership employees met out on the back stoop, slowly smoking their cigarettes, looking at every car. A small crowd had formed beneath the Kay Billboard, with people on lunch break joining his father's steely stare out at U.S. 23 North. David elbowed J.K. in the ribs when Sheriff Olson rolled up and parked on the shoulder of the two-lane highway, as he took in the scene. Neither boy bothered to hide—two kids playing hooky weren't on the sheriff's radar today.

Dietrich rolled up to the gate in the same lot as the van, passing by in his gleaming black Japanese cruiser and parking just feet from the padlocked fence. Kay appeared without prompting from the mechanics' station with Maurie on a leash. J.K. fought off David's grip and jumped out the passenger door. He ran to save his dog, to protect his family honor, but the handoff happened without protest from his dad: "This isn't even the same Maurie you gave us, Dee, it's his son."

"So much the better."

J.K. skidded to a stop as Dietrich opened the door and

Maurie climbed inside without a whimper, as though he were already at home. J.K. came up to Dietrich, ready to shout in the German's face, but the old man's sad eyes, as green as his own, made him shiver from the northerly wind, made him freeze in place as Dietrich shut the car door and rolled out of the gravel side lot, the dispersing crowd following him down the highway.

Only when David leaned out of the van to motion that they were late for English class, did J.K. even bother speaking to his father, who stood, padlock in hand, in a shock of his own.

"Dad, why in the hell did you give him Maurie?"

"Because I wasn't going to give him you."

This came as no surprise. Not really. J.K. had always known there was something strange in the love triangle that had dominated much of his family's drama. But it drained him to finally hear the words and he slumped over. He had been so dead-set on saving those around him that he had not been ready. Not for this. J.K. clutched his dad to keep from falling, while his other father disappeared along the road hugging the lake.

******* ******* *******

It wasn't long before the Japanese car was sold and replaced with a Ford pick-up truck from the Kay Dealership, still black, but no tinted windows, no shotgun rack.

Dietrich settled back in town, moving out of his apartment to a house on the north side to live close to Kay and his son. If the town thought anything of this, they were as silent as windless snow settling onto hilltops through double pane storm windows.

Kay and Dietrich settled back into their spots at the Owl Saloon, but at a booth near the window. On one side of the table that split the bar like a river, the German petted his dog, and the Pole slipped his beer to Junior for an occasional sip. J.K. felt the warm lager slide down him and he was filled with something. He hoped it wasn't gas, as he had plans to see Tracy later. Above them, holiday decorations matched the glow of the laughing clientele as Bing Crosby crooned Christmas ballads from Eva's stereo behind the bar.

Dietrich finished his drink and stood up. Kay snatched the mug from his son and hurried to catch up, gulping down the beer, reaching the bar at the same time as the German. An animated Eva came over to serve their need, dropping a towel between them onto a rivulet of ale that cascaded down the grooved bar.

J.K. stared at Maurie, who lapped at the last drops of beer in the puddle where Dietrich's glass had stood, and the dog stared back at him, both of them bristling with nervous energy. He fingered the spoon from his place setting and felt the pattern of roses along its spine. After a while, the cool metal turned the temperature of his hand, and Maurie moved to J.K.'s side of the table, resting his head on his lap.

J.K. waited for the old men who were his family to tire and for David's van to roll up so he could go off to some new party that night and smoke Parliaments and talk with husky-voiced girls at some hunting lodge or cottage. He would leave his coat and hockey mask behind and shiver in the wind dying in the breakers of pines so that he could whisper secrets to Tracy that none of his hockey buddies could hear.

GPS Love Affair

Every young man needs advice. This is a common sentiment among parents of arranged marriages. Dean was no exception. At first he was coolly indifferent to his new bride and her impressive dowry of unerring navigation, sultry voice, and macabre sense of humor. Her called her "Lovey" and his parents let him know that she was a sophisticated lady who'd been educated in the ways of the world. She definitely knew how to get her point across with a commanding voice and confidence that he hoped would rub off on him.

Dean allowed her to rule their wheeled roost with graceful efficiency. She offered up exotic cuisine when he was hungry and seemed to know which bars, strip clubs, and massage parlors would fulfill his needs. It was the way she ordered him around, however, that made him fall for her. She could sense his moods—she commanded him when he felt directionless on his path and was supportive when he was in the dumps with jokes about U-turns and crashing on dead-end streets.

There was something melancholy, though, in her lullabies at the end of each journey, and he found himself wondering if there had been anyone in her life before him. She did not seem to mind his own infidelities, putting up with his I-pod "Dovey" and his passion for his slim, sexy Bluetooth he kept close to him at all time. Once after a day and night of driving she told him about how her first relationship had lasted three years and had ended abruptly in a car crash that she blamed herself for to this very day.

After that confession, the end was inevitable, he supposed. She started pulling back from him, going through long periods of silence, and sending him into seedy sections of town. He wasn't certain what to make of it all until the day he came back from karaoke with his window smashed in. After all they'd been through, Lovey had run off with another man. In romance, he was used to losing out to bad boys and could not get her voice out of his head. He got depressed whenever he got lost in the city and even his parents were upset that their arrangement had not worked out.

After a time he stopped looking to see if he recognized her riding shotgun next to other drivers. But her voice stayed with him always. He heard her in the loudspeakers at department stores, in the commands of his boss on speakerphone, in the tinny murmur of dolls, clutched to chests. No one gets over a love such as this. In the klaxons of amber alerts and nuclear winter, she would be there to guide him into the darkness, the affairs of the earth.

Nick's Place

Dysfunction Junction. That's what we call the bar nestled among a stand of trembling aspens on the county road linking Yellowstone and Grand Teton national parks. The road's number is not important. It's a two-lane of beaten asphalt that looks older than it really is—with potholes for acne, skid marks for crow's eyes, and a shoulder no wider than a farmer's hamhocks. You've either navigated this road on your way to college, or thought it was quaint on a rustic trip to the country, or memorized every cranny as you've ridden it back and forth to a town barely large enough for its own post office.

Sometimes the road's driving you. Harder. Faster. The hum of tires spinning into infinity. Occasionally, you slow below the posted speed limit and note the words "Dysfunction Junction" on the back of a deer-crossing sign. Most of us at the bar figure the road marker was penned by Nick, old cougar that he was, marking his turf.

Nick the joker. Nick the quick. The scent of him is still all over his place. He built the L-shaped building that houses the bar with his own hands during the summer of '71 after his second tour in Nam. Everything—from the off-key piano in the bar's back room to the taped-up dog tags dangling on a nail above top-shelf whiskies—reminds us of him. Even the park rangers from Yellowstone and Teton. We can't look at their uniforms without remembering how they're responsible, partially at least, for our loss.

Sometimes, Nick's bar is better defined by what it lacks. He doesn't allow hats because of the helmet he boiled in following his Captain through pocked hamlets and rice fields with a PRC-77 radio strapped to his back. He told us the added weight was worth staying close to the man calling the shots—a quarter of his platoon fell in one battle alone. That also explains his ban on radios. The gurgle of static, he told us soon after his return, will drive any man nuts.

The real name of Dysfunction Junction is Nick's Place, but no one calls it that. Not since the incident that put our hangout on the map. At least, it made quite a splash in the local press: *The Cody Chronicle*, *The Thermopolis Tribune*, *The Sheridan Star*. One of the tabloids even sent a paparazzo to hound us. But we knew how to get rid of that fast-talking slicker, just as we do anyone who crosses us.

We aren't vindictive, but this bar means a lot to us. To some, it is family—or as close as we'll ever come to it. And like any family, there are rules and there are rules destined to be broken. And then there's the 17th parallel of rules, an action that carries irrevocable consequences. This particular line in the sand was crossed by the rangers earlier in the summer during one of the worst heat waves on record. It was mid-July, mid-afternoon, mid-bender for some of us. The sulfur stench from the hot springs and geysers clung to the scorched grass outside like a second layer of skin. Tourists crawled across the hillsides like fire ants at a picnic. No, more powerful—like the thousands of Oglala Sioux and Cheyenne braves who'd smothered Custer at nearby Bighorn.

A burly park ranger named Chris started the trouble by resting a whiskey and soda on top of the scratched piano in the back. He was just about to take his eight ball shot in a loud game of doubles between the Teton and Yellowstone rangers at the bar's seldom-used pool table. Nick's older brother Gus—who bartends five nights out of seven—exploded when he saw the pint glass sweating on his brother's prized piano. He swore a blue streak across the tavern. Chris told him to stuff it. Gus barreled out beneath the serving station, snatched the cue out of Chris's hands and started hacking away at the rangers milling in the back, a half-dozen in all, two of them women.

Then the rangers attacked and the regulars pummeled back and there were fists flying, bones cracking, skin ripping, blood spurting, shrieks and shouts and curses. Cubby—a long-time Hollywood bit actor who'd moved to the area a few years back—hid behind his stool, protecting his vaguely familiar good looks. Sweet, a suburban housewife turned trucker, pitched a ranger women through a window into the garbage-cluttered side lot. Hans smashed a bottle of Jim Beam over a Teton head and Sarah did her version of a flamenco dance on the rib cage of a Yellowstone ranger that Dave and Mack had felled. Finally, we routed the uniforms and threw them the hell out of Nick's, with Gus screaming and swinging and promising worse if they ever showed their faces again.

We went back inside and nursed our wounds, waiting for something, Nick's unlikely return perhaps. Those of us who've set down roots at Dysfunction Junction understand the false allure of traveling to the coasts for fame, love, and fortune. We know everything important in the world has already been discovered and forgotten. So we bide our time in the crannies of the nation's park lands, waiting for the awe and wonder we felt as children to return. We aren't sure whether it will open up like the glitter of a rare rock formation in a newly-discovered cavern or the fleeting nighttime blooms on a desert cactus. We just believe in the possibilities and each other—and for most of us that's enough.

******* ******* *******

The real story behind our attack on the rangers began a lifetime ago, or at least it must have seemed that way to Nick. He was a sturdy, good-natured kid growing up, the kind guys would pat on the back and women on the ass. But when he came back from Nam, some of the fire had gone from his eyes. What was left was a black wound in the center of his head, a slow smoldering, more coal than eyes, and we had no idea at first what might erupt from the depths of them…or him.

Before his tours, Nick had plans of leaving the woodland paths and stony fissures and boiled-egg musk of the geysers and traveling to New York, Europe, Japan. For art. For women. For adventure.

But after he came back, we never heard him mention those flights of fancy again, his face becoming as somber as the stone mugs on Rushmore. So Nick made himself useful by building his bar and watching over the drunks like a night patrol commander over rice paddies. Only we were the ones becoming soaked, over-ripened, spoiling on the vine.

Nick's vigilance never wavered. He kept himself to one

drink a night, a tall shot of whiskey just before closing time. We could set our watches by it. And so life went. A lot of drinking, a little farming, the occasional odd job, the people in these parts came and went. Nothing changed much. Until the day she came through the door.

Her name was Jen, that's what she called herself, but the name her tribe gave her was Gentle Hands. Or so she said. We were used to people shading their pasts as they wandered through haunted parklands that made idols out of murderers, collapsing landmarks, even the starving animals that ranged it. Depending on her stories and how much she drank, Jen was half Oglala Sioux or Cheyenne or Crow. The other half must have been pure devil, no smoldering in that one.

We joked that she and Nick were both veterans—he from Nam and she—her battlefield was inside of her. Unlike us, whose wounds were buried inside livers, kidneys, and lungs, Jen carried her pain like a match against the flint. Anger spewed out of her mouth with ashes and brimstone. Face like a statue, mouth like a gutter. She could tickle those ivories, though. She'd come in plowed and plunk herself down behind the piano. We'd belt out songs and get blasted, the wood walls breathing and pulsing from the life pumping inside of it. We lost ourselves in joy for awhile…reveling in Nick's happiness and Jen's lust. But like all good times, they weren't destined to last.

Nick was crazy about Jen. Hell, we all were. But she did everything a little too fast, lived a little too hard. To us drunks—whose centers of gravity made us more grounded and attached to our bar stools—it was obvious she was an addict. The signs weren't hard to spot, but Nick took a swing at anyone who bad-mouthed her.

He was going to ask her to marry him or so he confided to us, his long-faced troops. She was always saying how she wanted to run her body over America: the mountains, the rivers, the city streets, from plateaus to gutters. She wanted to spread herself over every curve of it and he promised he would help her. His long-forgotten itchiness for adventure took hold of him like a fever.

Uncharacteristically drunk one night, he confided that he was going to pop the question at the top of the Empire State Building, the tallest skyscraper in the world. None of us had the heart to tell him it wasn't the biggest any more.

So we gave them a going away party on a night where the moon hung low and yellow in the sky like a urinal cake. Jen was hammered and said we'd celebrate enough that night to make up for the rest of the summer they'd be gone. She was right, too. Jen and Nick didn't leave until almost sun-up, promising they'd just go a little ways and grab some shuteye before heading on.

It was about a week later when the strange sightings

started. Nick had gotten himself a Winnebago the color of a chestnut roan and personalized plates—JENNICK, a combination of their names. A soldering of letters that made about as much sense to us as how the rain and land joined together, transforming seeds into sprouts and sand into stone. A seamless joining that promised eternity—like co-mingled Native and settler blood seeped into red rock long ago.

People kept saying they saw this Winnebago rumbling around the parkland, sometimes in Montana, other times in Idaho, South Dakota, too. We thought it was funny, like a prairie ghost story or the Mystery Van from Scooby Doo.

Until we saw it with our own eyes.

It was closing time, late July, the biggest moon we ever saw. Gus kicked us out at closing time and we stayed outside awhile smoking and finishing up our beers. The Winnebago came weaving past us, throwing up gravel on the shoulder of the road. It was mud-splattered, dented, and humming along on bald tires. The license plate looked as if someone had tried ripping it off the bumper with bare hands...JENNICK peeking out from the twisted frame.

None of us could think of a good reason why Nick would be back and not stop in, so we called the police and notified the park staff. It was one of the rangers that found them, too. Parked in Teton at a weekly campsite. We knew we shouldn't hold a grudge against them for doing their jobs, but whenever we saw them…all we could think about is what they discovered and how it changed our lives.

****** ******* ******

Not long after our brawl with the rangers, on a summer afternoon that made even the shadows inside waver from the sun, they entered the bar and our lives with wide smiles and an absence of fear. Their names were Oscar and Izetta, although they went by Ozzie and Izzie like they were in a 50s sitcom or characters in a Salinger novel.

They were college students, they said, from Omaha, but their eyes told a different tale. When Gus carded them, Ozzie was quick to show he was 21, while Izzie wandered absently to the piano, running her hands along the keys too lightly to trip the hammers.

"We're in a band," Ozzie said, looking at the red lettering we'd put above the door one night. "Dysfunction Junction," he said. "Now that's a great name for us." Ozzie looked at Izzie, who ignored him, then ordered a draft for them to share as though he feared her absence, like when he followed her into the unisex john when she had to go.

Then there was the question of their car in the parking lot, a vintage Mustang that had known garages and suburbs its whole life before being driven hard along the Western trail by these souped-up kids.

When the car disappeared the next day, Ozzie said they'd sold it, although they had no more money afterwards than before, and we knew everyone in the area who might have bought it…and hadn't.

So Gus let them stay like so many of the drifters who had come before in the field behind the bar overgrown with weeds, stunted corn stalks, and wildflowers. They camped there with barely a sound and when they weren't with us, we looked to see if there was movement inside, our imaginations soused and the shadows ripe from the bar's yellow glow.

The kids spent weeks with us, sounding flighty and upbeat, talking about their dreams, but we knew they saw something of themselves in our red eyes and scarred hands. They planted themselves on the pair of bar stools in the corner where Nick and Jen had once sat, and their past was poured out to us slowly, like a bottle of tequila trying to hide its worm. It was obvious—they were running from something, just like we all were.

******* ******* *******

After finding Nick and Jen, Chris and his ranger pals had rolled into Dysfunction Junction with their customary swagger and a duty to tell us what had gone on. Apparently, one of the campers in Teton had complained about a smell coming out of the Winnebago. It rose up in the winds off the mesa bluffs and settled like a dark cloud

76

over the site. The campers thought it might be a dead cat, but it wasn't…it was Jen.

She'd overdosed on smack the first night they left. That's what Chris told us after hemming and hawing, explaining how Nick had been pacing at the foot of her bed, anxious to keep them from touching her where she was laid out—his rotting angel. The rangers laughed at that and Gus kicked them out of the joint, telling them to never come back.

And as for Nick? No charges were filed against him. We can thank semi-regular Sheriff Pellson for that. He took the heroin and flushed it down the bar john soon after dropping him back in our midst. Nick was out of his mind. In grief. In anger. In a lightless prison that was his eyes. It was almost like we didn't know him. At first, we wondered if he might not have been using himself, but his arms were clean, his legs were clean.

Nick got hammered his first night back like we hadn't seen him do since he was a teenager. He kept talking crazy shit, about how he'd promised to let Jen rub her body over the yellow prairie bluffs and that he still wanted to ask her to marry him on top of the world's tallest building…a building made of ash.

She lay in a coffin over at Clark's funeral home in Cody. We never did know what tribe she was from or her nearest kin. Nick kept insisting we were her family and convinced a couple of us to drive him over to see her—so he could pay his last respects. On the way, he cranked the radio and crooned over the staticky rock in a language seemingly without vowels.

Once we got there, he starting calling for Jen to come out. He scooped up gravel and flung it at the windows of the funeral home. At first, he was like a teenager trying to get his girlfriend's attention. Then the pebbles bounced harder on glass as he pitched them from behind the cover of his truck, and we ducked away from the rain of shrapnel. He ordered us to lower the bed of the pick-up so that we could take her with us.

He charged up the steps and kicked in the front door, all the while yelling for us to flank him, but we just couldn't. He wasn't quite able to get the coffin in the truck without our help. At the end, he laced his hands around his head in a helmet of flesh, and called out our coordinates for dust-off to the still-blaring radio.

The police came of course—hard not to with all the racket—and they took him away. He's in a home now...for people with problems accepting the way things are.

And it was then we knew if the country had a heart, it was made of stone, stone that sometimes cracked under the strain of great weights or boiled in underground geysers or turned to mush from the rain that had fallen through us.

****** ****** ******

A couple months after they showed up, icy-handed Ozzie and Izzie camped out at the bar on a night when a storm had turned them out of their leaky tent with gales and sputters.

They had been avoiding us for awhile, seeing the need in our eyes and too embarrassed for the charity we heaped on them. But that night they relented, and we bought rounds for the place one by one, getting everyone heated and squishy on the inside.

After a shot of rye ordered up by Sarah, Ozzie and Izzie moved to the piano. She played songs none of us had heard before and Ozzie played along with a mouth harp tuned to the wind whistling outside.

At first, we expected Gus to stop them, but he came back from behind the bar and pressed in the circle around them like the rest of us, leaving Sweet to dispense liquid cheer with her soft truck driver's hands.

After awhile, we learned the melodies and sang along like mountains breaking in two, bison rumbling across the plains in thundering herds, echoes of Native drums on the spine of the Black Hills.

We sang like there was no tomorrow and, of course, tomorrow came.

Just before midnight, a stranger slipped through the

doors with a city accent, polished shoes, a worn suit, and a bulge in his coat that told us everything we needed to know. He was a gun for hire, a dead-eyed detective.

Behind him followed a man that wore the grief of fatherhood as closely as the rain poncho that clung to his skin. "Izetta," he said to her, and she froze at the keyboard.

"And you," he growled at Oscar, "she's only sixteen."

And the private dick lurched toward Ozzie, who sidled away from the bench, but the sight of Sheriff Pellson at the bar stopped him and the P.I. both. What happened next is a matter of park lore.

The boy flew like the thirteenth blackbird or Thelma and Louise in perpetual drift across the Grand Canyon.

In three impossibly long running steps, Ozzie launched himself from the piano bench, flew over the pool table and the pitcher of Bud at Dave and Mack's table, and dove perfectly out the windows, whose fresh glass from the ranger incident shattered like thunder.

What happened next—the footsteps disappearing into the night, the father's tears as he clutched his baby, the water that flowed from the wound in the bar across the dusty floor—was like a cleansing, a cold draft piercing through us all.

Of course we had seen many crazy nights over the years, but this one came at us filled with joy, then grief, and all the weight of a slow-moving storm that would not abate. A few of the regulars cried after the kids were gone and the weaker ones clung to the stronger, and no one drank another drop, although it was an hour to closing.

****** ****** ******

After that evening, the regulars erected a new sign for NICK'S PLACE atop the bar, then disbanded for awhile. We went back home to make amends with scattered loved ones, long-shelved friends, and estranged relatives. Gus even made a trip to visit Nick at the state home in Billings. It went well, we suppose. He spends fewer shifts at the bar. We know that Nick will return in time...but we have all the time in the world.

So we continue on with our small talk and our small lives in one of America's forgotten hollows, tucked away between jagged ridges and unending prairie. The sky's belly hangs so low we can pocket the clouds by day and harvest the stars at night. We never mention the incident just as we do not speak about the young couple that passed through. It doesn't take much in the way of brains to figure out they provided us with a wake...but one for the living, for Nick, for wounds eventually healing. But then again, if you think about it, wakes are always for the living, just as wars—even unpopular ones or those long forgotten—can bring the touch of death to gentle hands.

In the Dark

"So, you're saying if I stick my tongue in the outlet, this light bulb will glow?"

Nicki nodded, wondering how mad her dad would get if he knew they were alone together again.

"I don't believe you," he said, setting down the bulb they'd taken out of the reading lamp. Larry was seven, like her, but seemed younger by his willingness to do whatever she asked. Like running around the playground in his underwear or eating tree bark or the time dad found them in the basement alone playing with their "thingees."

They'd both gotten spanked for it, but hadn't complained.

"How come you don't talk to me in school anymore," Larry asked.

"It's because we have a special relationship. Do your mom and dad talk?"

"Oh," Larry said, "So this is better?"

"Of course it is," Nicki said. "We'll do dangerous things, then we'll fight about it."

"OK."

Nicki picked up a letter opener and grabbed Larry's hand. She kissed him on the lips and knelt down by the outlet. The hair on her neck was already beginning to rise. She pushed the opener into the outlet prong but it was too big. She hated Larry. He would ignore her if she didn't ignore him.

"Nicki," her father called out from the living room. Their parents must be looking for them.

"Quick," Nicki said, breathless. Hand in hand, they held the bulb and hid in the closet of the den, wondering if their bodies huddled together would trigger the light and cause her dad to find them.

In the dark, Larry wasn't a boy and she wasn't a girl. They were the same.

"I'm scared," Larry said.

"Me too," said Nicki, but she wasn't scared, not even as they met the future with open mouths and the calls grew louder and her father's footsteps slowly approached their hiding place.

Stone Feathers

"Some stones believe they're statues and some statues that they're gods."

Last week, at a Republican fund raiser, a washed-up politico—after wolfing three éclairs—had burst into tears, then into this off-key song about statues. What bothered Dick most was that he himself had crooned these words, much to the chagrin of his friends and staff. He had never heard such unmitigated horseshit before, not even from the press.

Nixon sighed and crossed his hotel suite, opening the double French doors to the balcony overlooking the capitol. He would never have believed himself capable of such overblown sentimentality until last month when, bombarded by the none-too-subtle hints of his advisors, he began monitoring himself on tape. Video *and* audio this time. Son of a bitch. It was all there in black and white, and depending on the TV, all the muted colors of gray-suited skies, red power ties, and curtained night.

What had happened to his nerve?

He feared the song escaping his lips was trumpeting a personal Jericho, like the graffitied slabs of East Berlin tumbling into vendors' arms, the forces of war and deception he'd set in motion years before, or an epitaph he'd stenciled onto his own tombstone and smashed so many times that he no longer knew what it said, or the realization, on mornings like this when all the money in the world could not buy a decent breeze off the beltway, that the women in his life were dead. All except Patricia, who treated him as though he were a small child to be chided or a lance to be boiled.

Hell, even the wind was giving him the silent treatment today. He turned his back to the indifferent cityscape and stepped inside the presidential suite of the Royal Victoria Hotel. It was an important day, he reminded himself, examining his morning's shave in the bureau vanity. Someone important had died. He'd forgotten who, but somehow that seemed unimportant. The funeral would happen with dignitaries and 21 guns and political graybeards quivering with the irrefutable knowledge that their times were near.

Nixon stared in the looking glass beneath his crooked

nose and wrinkled eyes, imagining he was garbed in purple robes like Richard the Lion Hearted, or that he donned a fool's cap splayed with bells like Loki the God of Mischief. Yes, this was an important day to regain old ground. If he could only last another fifteen or twenty years, he knew that he could recast himself as an elder statesman or an iron-willed ruler who'd thwarted war. Even Loki had had seven incarnations to make his mark, and had been hardened enough to swallow the heart of the woman he loved so that he could bear a son.

Much like today's politicians who carve the hearts of prince and pauper to feel the pain of their constituents, and then turn to ad men, those esteemed poets, to fill the empty chests of those who once believed in Jefferson and Lincoln. Hey...that wasn't half bad. He should get hold of his assistant Money and let her in on his latest flash of wisdom. He dragged his stiff right leg across the austere and (to his specifications) uncluttered suite to the black and gold rotary phone on his nightstand.

He paged his assistant Money (not her real name of course, but she didn't seem to mind the nickname) and limped back to the marble-tiled balcony. His rooster, moored by tape and twine to his right leg, clucked and whined from not having breakfast, but Dick stamped his foot and the beast quieted. This weathered fowl was always with him, ravenous, a warrior. It first appeared in a dream during the final months of his presidency, and had gained more substance each year since. It despised the artifices of diplomacy and saw the world in chessboard hues of black and white. Although it was invisible to everyone else, he knew it was as real as he was, perhaps more so.

Dick didn't mind the company or the unclouded perspective the beast gave him. Although his assistant's diaries and the desire to publish them furthered his own ends, his rooster knew Money for the parrot she was, and squirmed within its restraints to swallow the bird whole. Nixon paced from banister to banister, and the motion seemed to quell his bird of prey. He peered out over the balcony at the land he'd once ruled. The autumn day was non-distinct and gray, the cloverleaf swollen with human cattle grazing for greenbacks. And all the cowboys hired to watch them were inside, nestled from the smog in their mausoleums of stone.

******* ******* *******

Money chewed her bottom lip, stifling the laughter bubbling up inside her. "Very good, Mr. Nixon, very graphic...politicians as modern-day vampires."

"Thanks. I thought you might like it."

"Very profound. Will there be anything else?"

"Could you make sure Cook takes proper precautions for my lunch with Bill?"

"What's the caterer's name again?"

"Roy, from Royburgers. I don't like fried foods myself, but Clinton does...."

"Gotcha," Money said, departing the mammoth room. And not a moment too soon. Dick was in a pisser of a mood and she didn't like his recent penchant for walking around without clothes. Like he was now. She thought he was keen and wise, and all that, but he wasn't the cutest guy who ever lived. Major historical figures rarely were: English royalty, Hitler, Napoleon.

She slid the suite door shut, leaving the big guy hanging out over the balcony. Before tracking down Cook, she decided to record their latest conversation. She plopped in a chaise lounge outside the oak door, unsnapped her purse and whipped out her leather-bound diary. She knew that Dick monitored her journals, but since he was paranoid with friends and family, she took it as a sign of esteem and affection. Or at least attention, which she didn't mind.

Her fingers trailed down the India black swoops of her oversized, but flawless cursive. When she wrote about her Nixonic adventures she made sure to use the quill that Dick had given her last Christmas. He'd told her the pen had been made from the feather of a Dodo, who, like Democrats, once numbered in the millions and would eventually see the same end. She uncapped the inkbottle, dipped the tip of the flat tan feather into the well, and flipped her diary to last night's entry, which pieced together the most recent fragments of the big guy's song.

Some stones believe they're statues
 and some statues that they're gods.

She didn't quite know what to make of the lyrics. She thought they might be important, but didn't know if they would fit into the best-seller she was planning to write, a book that would cast the big guy in a good light and herself in a much better one. History wasn't about truth, she'd decided, but about telling the best story. If she had the skill to recast Dick as a domesticated wolf or wronged nobleman, people would start forgetting the history books and newsreels, and embrace the fable. Her reinvention.

A horrible scraping on the Victorian hardwood next door sent her scrambling to her feet. What was that sound? A chicken? Or was it the old man coughing? She snatched up her feather and felt a prick in her palm from the quill point as she scrambled to get out of there before Dick caught her sloughing off.

Despite her plans, she really cared what he thought of her. As he did of her. She knew he craved the admiration and respect she showed him. He'd gotten a bogus rap was all, like her parents had given her because she was the youngest and a girl. She knew what it was like to claw and scratch her way up, and she'd be damned if she was going to feel sorry for the saps in the world who didn't have her talent or drive or will to succeed. She would show them what she was made of. Just like her mentor. Just like the damn dodos. She would show the world.

******* ******* *******

Cook caught his reflection in the chrome stove handle and adjusted his white chef's hat so that it accentuated his blond bangs. If there was one thing he'd learned from working for the rich, it was that looking the part was every bit as important as what lingered beneath the window dressing. The same applied to the glazes and garnishes that accompanied his recipes, although Dick's taste tended toward the pedestrian, if not the occasionally bizarre. Like the ketchup and cottage cheese phase that had led to the departure of the chef before him.

Cook sharpened his cutlery and eyeballed Money as she swiveled in a bar stool next to the sink. He scowled and tried to appear menacing, but Money was never one to take a hint. She alternated between scribbling in a leather-bound diary and making inane chitchat.

Money sighed and glanced at her watch. "Christ, like I don't have better things to do than wait around for you to get your act together."

"Then don't. When I'm ready, I'll go down and escort the burger man up here myself."

"That's the difference between you and me, Cook. When Dick asks me to do something, I follow his instructions to the letter."

"All his instructions, I imagine."

"What's that supposed to mean? For someone who dresses as meticulously as you do, you spend a lot of time with your mind in the gutter."

"Just thinking about you," Cook said innocently.

"Whatever. Can't you speed things up? The burger guy has been waiting over a half hour with the Secret Service."

"Like I care."

Trouble was, Cook actually did care that he wasn't preparing one of Dick's cross-ideological favorites like Kung Pao Pizza, but he wasn't about to tell that to Money. She actually thought they were bosom buddies. OK, so she wasn't the most annoying person who ever lived, but she was always grilling him about Tricky D. And she was constantly underfoot in the kitchen, like now, which was even worse in this blasted hotel kitchenette.

"OK, hon, bring him back. Everything's as ready as it's going to get.

"It's not like you're cooking today."

Cook gripped a spatula, cocked his arm, and Money bolted toward the lobby. The brat played dumb, but she could be pretty wry sometimes. He continued scrubbing the already-spotless counter and steeled himself to watchdog the burger man. Tricky D had taken him into his confidence about his recent strange behavior. Too much sugar threw the former pres out of whack, made him do silly things and black out. The doctors weren't sure what the problem was—they didn't think it was diabetes—but Cook made sure to monitor what Dick ate. That was no easy task either, the way the old dog craved sweets.

Cook was, admittedly, too intimidated to talk to the former president about his worrisome behavior. Just this morning Dick had asked for a chicken and egg omelet with the simple explanation, "Mothers and daughter together as one."

Even now Cook could feel the goose bumps on his arms. To kill time while Chef Roy cleared security, Cook picked up the phone to see if the hotel staff had mended the old man's favorite suit yet. The right knee kept wearing through, almost as though Dick had taken up prayer.

******* ******* *******

Two globs of pink meat sizzled on Roy's burger-crusted griddle. Cook felt nauseous from the smoke and the globs of fat popping in oil.

"Bacon grease, that's the real reason why they keep coming back," Roy told him proudly.

"So how many presidents have eaten these…burgers?"

"Every single one from the time of Teddy Roosevelt. My grandpa Roy owned the business then."

"Everyone except for Nixon, you mean?"

"Yep, he always thought I was out to kill him with cholesterol. All the presidents had their specialty, too. Green tomatoes for Carter. Pine nuts for Truman. All except Bill, who likes trying everyone else's concoction. And now Nixon's asking for a turkey burger, calling it America's most patriotic bird of prey. What the hell's that supposed to mean?"

Cook shook his head solemnly, sadly, as leaned back against the counter. Dick was in rare form today. Maybe that explained why the old man had ordered his turkey burger rare.

Even now he Cook could feel his cooking skills atrophy, while the pores on his face clogged with grease. The things he went through to work for the rich and famous. It would pay off someday, though. He would own his own DC bistro and cater to the politicians and their cronies, offering them discounts and laughing at their political in-jokes. He would become a household name. Maybe even land a syndicated cooking show with a snazzy name like The Deacon of Dining.

Roy poked Cook in the ribs. "You OK, son?"

"Yeah, I'm fine. Smells…hmm…tasty. Must be good cuts of meat."

"Damn straight. The real secret, though, is that we slit these babies' throats ourselves on my brother's farm and cart 'em in to the city almost before their hearts stop beating."

******* ******* *******

Bill tried to hide his impatience with his host's ramblings. Dick had proved to be a boon to him in the area of foreign relations, but he was off kilter today, distracted, as though there were a ghost darting in and around his hotel suite. Besides, he didn't like the look of the mousy assistant who kept interrupting their meeting to whisper long passages in Dick's ear, all the while staring at him with a shy-but-not grin. It smelled like trouble. It felt familiar and scary and exciting.

"Someone's died again. It's going to be an important day," Dick said with all the excitement of a schoolboy dragged to Sunday mass.

"Important, yes, and yet very sad. He was, after all, a great man," Bill said, even as he found himself wondering if Dick was taking either too much prescription medication or too little. Maybe it was the funeral that was getting to him. Heaven knew the former president had had his share of misfortune lately. Bill chewed thoughtfully on his Kennedy Burger and sucked on the grilled onions before swallowing. Great added touch. Spicy. Flavorful. Something. It was always those intangibles that separated the Kennedy era from Dick's or even his own.

He took another hearty bite and watched Dick nibble at the pickle on his plate. A slight well of blood trickled from his friend's untouched turkey patty and, for a split second, Bill wondered if there was a tasty heart, blackened with grease, wasting away beneath the bun. He licked his lips and felt something bump his leg beneath the table. Dick bared his teeth, stomped his feet and gnawed on his pickle spear like he had to make it last a thousand years. Had Nixon gotten himself a puppy? Bill opened his mouth to ask, but Dick's expression stopped him cold.

****** ******* ******

Money knew the politicians around her were making up their own stories as they went. It didn't matter if you were outlandish in your claims, just that you were confident and believed in what you were saying. What was hearsay today would become mythic tomorrow. There were some American ideals which were only kept alive in TV commercials: mothers making their children lunches, teenagers playing Twister, happy frat boys squeezing into phone booths.

While the former and current presidents had lunch under the gaze of Cook, Roy, and twitchy Secret Service men, she imagined a different story altogether. The King's son William had taken over the kingdom, but didn't like that his father was more famous than he was. He plotted to kill him by poisoning him slowly. With lunches. With sweets. By stirring up the old man's heart with foreign policy blunders. She could hear the son's laughter in the next room while her quill danced in her hand, staining her notebook. She felt certain, somehow, that these thoughts would survive them all, like the feather in her hand had survived the dodo.

******* ******* *******

Dick's stomach rumbled from the lack of food. He was having a hard time keeping himself in check. The heavily-restrained rooster on his leg wanted to scarf up the chameleon on the podium even while Bill spoke of the great man's deeds. The rest of the rogue's gallery was there to hog the spotlight: Jimmy, Jerry, George, Nancy, even fucking Mondale. He hadn't been able to stomach these dog and pony shows since his wife passed away.

Money kept trying to steer him into reporters after the 21-gun salute. He knew he should try to further his media resurrection, but couldn't concentrate. The ceremony had left him cold and he really didn't feel like posing for posterity. The old guard was passing away and all of them would soon only be historical footnotes, some larger than others, but inevitably their stardom destined to fade in the twilight of ink on page.

Dick was one of the first to filter into the West Wing and eye the buffet spread. He whisked past the hors d'oeuvre and cheese plates, and hurried to a small tin of brownies beneath a miniature American flag, it too at half mast.

His rooster dug in its spurs and hissed, but stopped when Dick swallowed the first square whole. His turkey lunch, heavy with the fear of a conquered bird, had not been enough to fill him…would never be enough. A second brownie followed, then a third.

A warm glow started in the center of his chest and spread outward. His fingers were no longer cold. Spots of dark and light swam before him, tingeing the dusk in a shadowy film. Everyone turned and stared at him, eager to hear him speak. From across the room, Money shook her head vehemently and took a step toward him, her manicured fingers balling into a fist that looked like it could fell kingdoms, an army of pressmen, a tired old man. The rooster on his leg, for the first time he could remember, was scared.

He cleared his throat and crooned, *"Some stones believe they are statues and some statues that they're gods."*

Flushed, he barreled into a wave of incoming VIPs and stumbled to his knees. Dick clutched the pleated hem of a woman's dress, his leg burning.

Across the room Money was already in damage control mode. It was clear what she would say. The tired old king was praying, actually praying. He had taken the loss of the great man way too hard.

And as Money gave her interview, orioles and robins warbled in the bows of an ancient oak on the West Lawn. She listened to the songbirds just as they did her, and neither knew what the other was saying. Perhaps they didn't even understand themselves or, maybe, they were lonely or praying or cajoling for attention. Perhaps they wanted to nest in her bosoms or peck out her eyes. Perhaps all songs of longing were the same.

Hunter's Point

The first block Max felt nothing but guilt, his arms pumping like pistons, feet pounding, lungs burning, wishing he hadn't left Dario's toolbox outside where it could be plucked by anyone with a devious nature and a good pair of wire cutters. Beside him, Dario cursed in Spanish that would have sent his mother to confession, rosary in hand. In front of them, the thief streaked down the poorly paved street, red toolbox bouncing against his thighs, his shaved head rocking like a metronome. "Stop, thief!" Max yelled to the overcast dusk blanketing Hunter's Point, embarrassed he sounded like a flatfoot from a '70s detective show.

The second block seemed to take forever as they hit the base of a steep San Francisco rise, each upward stride as long as the silence between outbursts when he and his ex-girlfriend Beth fought. As they gained altitude, the closed Naval Base jutted into view alongside Dario's rented lot—the tin warehouse where they cranked out counterfeit *South Park* and *Simpsons* T-shirts, the abandoned school bus where Dario let Max stay for free after he got kicked out of his Mission flat, and the gray expanse of asphalt in between. Dario's curses turned to coughs and wheezes up the sharp incline. Max's bike messenger's calves screamed as he pulled even with Dario, the thief stepping off into a bank of fog over the crest. Max followed with a childish fear the sky would open up and swallow him whole.

The third block was like a gunshot in the air above a New Year's crowd, wild and impetuous, Max's feet slapping the poorly paved down slope as they closed the gap. It reminded him of what he loved best about cycling in and out of traffic, the rush and blare of horns kicking you into a steady buzz of adrenaline and escape. Beth had always liked that he was reckless. Dario, too, egged him on, screaming, "Push it, Max" as the kid began to tire, shifting the mechanic's box to his left arm and stumbling, losing ground.

The fourth block Max felt a sharp pain in his side, but he'd gotten used to discomfort—sleeping in a drafty bus on a single mattress, with a circular hole by the emergency door he used to relieve himself when he was too tired to make his way to the bathroom in the shed. Shivering alone at night he found himself drawn to the hard metal shell of the bus and the magnetic attraction for all things cold and hard: sheet metal walls, razors, bullets in the guns that fired off in the distance, beckoning him to follow their flight.

The fifth block they were almost on the thief's heels as they neared the bottom of the hill ending in a cul-de-sac. Dario whooped, but Max felt a vague dread, like during nightly calls with Beth when she gave him an update on the creature in her belly that had grown steadily to resemble, in no particular order: *a nut, a reptile, a rat, a chicken, a mutant* wiggling in ultrasound, each stage prompting her to comment, "He reminds me of you, Max." The boy lowered his head and lumbered down the driveway to a three-story housing project, one Dario and Max had often talked about, but had never gotten close to before.

Dario sprinted ahead like a man possessed, narrowing the gap. Max felt an overwhelming urge to hightail it out of there, every muscle in his body rebelling against the weakening signals from his brain. But, as he'd recently discovered, some memories refused to remain safely stored in a closet like a well-worn pair of tennis shoes that would never again handle a fast sprint or a dime turn.

On the yellow lawn of the housing project, the thief braked before Dario could jump him. He held out his arms and dropped the toolbox onto the sidewalk, saying, "Whoa, cool it."

Dario bent over double, heaving for air. Max felt suddenly cold. Long shadows had sprung up out of nowhere, the sun dipping behind the hilltop. Max looked up at the stairwells and windows of the cement complex. Their voices had drawn people to their doorways. They looked down with a cold expression that reminded Max of his own father—a stranger's mistrust. He wanted badly to escape, but he was tired of running and had learned the hard way as a kid to be stoic, no matter the danger.

"What're you waiting for? Take the damn thing back, if it's so important," the thief said, throwing up his hands.

"Damn right I will," Dario said. "What did you think you were doing? I work for my money, asshole."

Dario walked up face-to-face with the backing kid. "You have some kinda nerve." Max saw shadows skirt along the stairwell down toward the courtyard. "I came to this shitty neighborhood because the rent was low." A group started to form at the foot of the building stairwell. "But not nearly as low as the neighbors." A murmuring of angry voices.

"Come on, Dario, let's get out of here," Max said, even though he didn't have the slightest fear for his own safety. Still, it felt like life or death inside his chest.

"Not until this shit says he's sorry," Dario demanded.

The kid's eyes darted around the courtyard, trying to figure out how to save face. Max recognized the look;

it was the same expression he saw every morning while brushing his teeth in the tool shed—tunnel eyes set on oblivion. Beneath, Max could tell the kid wanted to bolt every bit as much as he had run from Beth or his mom had from his father.

"What's it going to be?" Dario growled.

But there are some things you can't flee from. Hide from. Ignore. Max stepped forward and yelled "Hey," and as Dario turned, Max hit his friend in the solar plexus with a stiff undercut. Dario staggered and fell on his ass in the brown grass, his mouth small and gasping. The thief darted off around the corner of the building and several onlookers broke out in laughter. "Crazy white boy," one said, but Max felt incredibly sane. He picked up the toolbox with one hand and helped Dario to his feet with the other. For once, his friend was at a loss for words.

He rested his hand on Dario's shoulder and guided him up the incline toward home. The only way to help his friend had been to hurt him. He looked at his knuckles, bruised from a recent fall from his bike. *Be tough, never cry*, the manly voice was still there in his ear. And yet, he ached. Inside. From how much he would injure Beth with this unspoken confession: *I'm afraid I'll harm my son like my father hurt me.*

As they reached the hilltop, Dario started to swear softly under his breath. Max figured it was a good sign—

his friend's pride was bruised worse than his ribs, but at least he was alive. Finally, Dario got back his wind and started laying into Max, saying, in no particular order: *"You're a nut, a rat, a chicken, a reptile, a mutant* no one wants around."

The sun sank lower into the ocean's belly and Max shivered in the breeze atop Hunter's Point, staring at the breakers for a sail cutting through the fog or anything solid in the murk. From the top of the rise, above the thieves and con men, he almost felt as though he could reach through the cloudbank with trembling hands and cradle a rising moon as faraway and magnetic as a new-born son.

Mosquito Island

The Bridge

I was four years old…maybe five. I remember geese rushing at me to snatch breadcrumbs from my fingers. Me screaming. Tossing the clumps of bread skyward. My mother using my body to shield her as those strange Michigan snowflakes fell out of season. My father laughing, telling me not to be such a baby.

It's funny which memories stick in your mind like boiled spaghetti to the kitchen wall or pencil marks charting an only child's growth on a doorjamb. The duck pond with its waterway leading to a grassy crest. The horseshoe driveway where teenagers park on dates. The inlet protected from passing motorists on U.S. 23 North by an overgrown stand of trees. A tiny bay swirling Lake Huron waters around a spit of land called Mosquito Island, separated from the town of Alpena by a short plank bridge.

It felt like walking the plank, too, the first time I stepped foot on that creaking wooden crosswalk. My mother and I have always had the same phobias: bridges, heights, insects, planes. "Go ahead, Scott, it's perfectly safe," my father told me, his high German forehead crinkled with impatience.

I closed my eyes and raced across the bridge, screaming in terror and exhilaration. I sprinted onto the island, down a dirt path and kept running. The sound of my name boomed like a cannon shot, then ceased, replaced by my father's racing footsteps. Christ, how he hated chasing after me.

Bird Call

Pretend you are a red-breasted robin pausing for a rest on a stump next to the only picnic table on Mosquito Island. Now imagine that a surly nine-year-old named Scott hurls a stone at you, forcing you skyward. You soar quickly above ten acres of sparse forest surrounded by a thin swirl of lake water. You wing south toward the only man-made object on the island—a one-story structure, oblong, made of cement. You're about to settle on the roof when several sharp crackles scare you airborne.

Inside the unmarked building is a rifle range. Teams

from local businesses are firing pistols and rifles in marksmanship competitions. Scott's father is there, representing the Phillips Cement team. The walls are supposed to be soundproofed, but gun blasts leak through cracks in the waterlogged foundation. You know enough not to nest near it. You rise swiftly above the town of Alpena, high enough to see Thunder Bay wash into Lake Huron.

You note the smokestacks, the stench of burnt maple syrup swirling from the saw mill, fishing trolleys and sailboats skimming summer currents, a storm cloud of limestone ash drifting westward from the cement plant where a thousand townspeople work, Carpenter's Bridge that spans an inlet awash with brown trout and walleye.

Then you swoop back down to your nest on the north end of Mosquito Island and settle on a tree branch above where the boy and his mother sit. They eat sandwiches and potato chips. He drinks a Coke. She pulls a beer free from a ringlet of six. When he's done with his can, he reaches over and starts drinking hers. She notices him stealing sips, but doesn't say a word. They stay for an hour or so, drinking and laughing, until the slow footfalls of the father signal that it's time to go home.

Soaking

I never visited Mosquito Island by myself until the time I ran away from home. I was eleven and my father was furious that I was still wetting the bed on almost a nightly basis. He'd tried everything to cure me. Punishing me with a belt, rigging an alarm to blare when the rubber sheets got wet, forbidding me from drinking anything after dinner. Public humiliation was the only course he had left to try, he told me one Saturday morning.

He gave me the bad news in a whisper; my father was the kind of man who never raised his voice. He could send me and my mother scrambling with the clearing of his throat. He instructed mom to hang my pee-stained sheets outside my bedroom window which overlooked State Avenue, the busiest street in town. My mother looked sorry for me, but knew better than to say anything, at least right away.

My father headed down to the basement on one of his marathon projects and my mother waited for me to stop crying and for her to finish a beer before following him downstairs. It wasn't like I'd wanted to wet the bed, for Christ's sake. I began gathering every off-limit item I could think of—a pack of my dad's Winstons, a bottle of Wild Turkey, a bag of semi-sweet chocolate chips, a package of pepperonis from the fridge. I stuffed the booty in my school backpack, stormed out the back door, and jumped on my bicycle.

Before long, I found myself on the north end of Mosquito Island, nestling in a small nook of tree roots by the duck pound and stuffing my face with chocolate, lunchmeat, and cigarette smoke. By the time I started in on the whiskey, I was sick as a dog. I puked my guts out in the water, drawing several Mallards that feasted on the spoils.

While leaning out from shore, I lost my step and stumbled into the shallows. My shoes and socks were sopping, and my shorts were soaked in the crotch. Of course, it wasn't long before a friend of my dad's happened across my hiding place with his wife and three daughters in tow. I jumped on my bike and sped toward home, but not before I saw a confused look register on the guy's face as he tried to fathom a drunken eleven-year-old with a wet spot on the front of his shorts.

When I got back home my folks didn't even notice I'd been gone or maybe they didn't care. I did catch hell, though, when the chocolate chips were clocked as missing. The folks drank so much they didn't even notice that the Wild Turkey had disappeared from the liquor warehouse they kept in the pantry by the fridge. I did manage that summer to finally stop wetting the bed. I'm not sure whether it was from fear of punishments my father would dole out or the coffee beans I started sucking at night to keep myself from sleeping.

Deer Season

My father was a storm cloud throughout my teenage years—brooding and stern, dark eyes flashing, voice like faraway thunder. Gradually, he began spending more time with his pals at the hunting lodge even when nothing was in season, or at the rifle range on Mosquito Island, or else at the Elk's lodge downing dollar drafts and charbroiled burgers from the grill. At night, I took my father's place in the living room easy chair beside my mother and fixed myself whiskey and Cokes, keeping her company in front of the TV. We'd joke and get blasted—the mood in our house lightened considerably without the old man.

I could swear she knew that I was making myself a drink every time I brought her a beer from the fridge. She would have to be blind not to notice my flushed cheeks and slurred speech. We would both get tired from the booze and struggle to make it through the ten o'clock line-ups of the major networks. I would go into school with wicked hangovers and make excuses for it by telling my teachers that I had a rare blood disease called Wilturcokolia that made me anemic and tired. They either bought it or else didn't want to know more about my home life. My dad, like many in Alpena, believed what went on in people's homes was nobody's business but their own.

Even when tragedy struck. When the news about my father's death arrived one chilly October night, I half expected to hear that a drunken hunter had blown his brains out. It was nothing quite so dramatic. He'd keeled over face first into a pile of plastic chips at the hunting lodge, clutching four queens and an 8. "It was the damnedest thing," I would hear his pals say for years afterwards.

It was the damnedest thing, too…I wasn't sure how I felt about his heart attack. Underneath, I wondered if my mother was as ambivalent as I was.

First Love

Tanya was a Polish beauty with light-brown hair and pale skin, who smelled faintly of cigarette smoke and her mother's mail-order perfume. She lived a block away from us on the Lake Huron side of State Avenue with a plumber for a father and a former Alpena Junior Miss for a mother. We became friends during the same mile and a half walk home from Alpena High School. She told me I was like the brother she never had. I told her she was closer than a sister, and God help me for the unbrotherly thoughts that crossed my mind on almost a nightly basis.

Our meandering route home from school took us past the duck pond and Mosquito Island. We would stop off at the island for a smoke, sitting on a stump that overlooked the pond, the top few floors of the county hospital visible above the tree line. When winter came and the leaves fell, I would take her further back into the bare trees, out of sight, hoping for something romantic to happen.

It never did. At least, not with her. Years later, I

brought my college girlfriends home to visit and took them for make-out sessions on the island. Partially, it was out of necessity. I always felt too guilty to sleep with someone in my mother's house. So I would bring my lovers to the wilds of my childhood and make love to them on those overgrown paths as I had never done with Tanya. The mosquitoes stung or else it was cold, but nothing hurt quite as much as the fact that I could never get over my feelings for her.

First loves are always like this, I suppose. Unrequited desire imprints itself in our teenage years, leaving a sadness that lingers even when in the arms of someone else. Throughout high school, I confided my feelings for Tanya to my mother who would hound me for details about the girls I was interested in and pick apart the few I mentioned. Mom and I were close after my father died. Maybe, too close. We talked about our days, traded jokes during bad TV sitcoms and played marathon games of Scrabble, Yahtzee, and cribbage. I was too embarrassed to tell her that she was my closest friend.

Like many best friends, we had a falling out. One I've never spoken about, not even to my wife, Jolene. One Friday evening mother and I stayed up late playing cribbage. She'd had a fight with her boss Ted at the car dealership, where she worked as a bookkeeper. She was plowed by the time we finished our third game and the subject of sex came up. "You're fifteen, plenty old enough," she said with a strange glint in her eye. She asked me if I'd perused the paperback romances she kept in her bedroom. I denied it at first, but she knew better. She'd noticed books that were missing, misfiled, dog-eared.

My curiosity was nothing to be ashamed about, she told me. "I'm going to do you a favor, one you'll thank me for later."

She disappeared upstairs and returned with an unmarked videotape. I don't know what I was expecting when she started the VCR, but certainly not what flashed next on the TV screen. The camera faded in on a young couple making out feverishly on their living room sofa, their hands everywhere at once. They stripped down to their underwear before they noticed a blonde nurse spying on them from the apartment across the street. Knowing they were being watched only turned them on more.

The dark-haired couple stripped and he took one of her erect nipples in his mouth. The man's penis was huge. His wife leaned over and began sucking on the tip of it. My own cock strained at the seams of my jeans. "Go ahead, it's OK," my mother said, nodding at my crotch. "Play with yourself." My eyes darted from the screen to my mother who breathed heavily and whispered, "You're turning into a man so quickly."

I pushed myself off the couch and hurried toward my

bedroom, shutting and locking the door. I sat on the edge of my bed, disgusted, excited, confused. Moans continued from the television for the next twenty minutes or so, during which time I masturbated and was working on a second time when the set shut off. I froze as I heard my mother's footsteps pause by my door before heading upstairs to her room.

The next day, we pretended that nothing had happened, but it had. In one fell swoop, we'd become as close and as distant as any mother and son could be.

The Skids

After the incident with the video, my mother and I lived separate lives. She turned to the bottle for comfort. I kept away from her as much as possible, invading Tanya's house for dinner and homework. She let me spend the night sometimes in her bed, both of us fully clothed with thick flannel sheets between us. I stopped going home except to take a shower, grab some food, and change clothes. Mom was getting smashed earlier and earlier. I decided when I turned 18 I would move out. "To make things easier on her," I told my friends, but it was to keep myself from joining her on the icy slopes of depression.

So Tanya became my surrogate family—would-be sister,

lover, and mother rolled into one. She and I spent so much time together everyone in high school assumed we were an item. I did nothing to stop the rumors. We were certainly caught in enough compromising situations. It had nothing to do with love, just a love of getting fucked-up.

When Tanya and I were old enough to drive our parents' cars, we would skip classes with her friend Karen or one of my pals from the hockey team. We'd go to Mosquito Island or the graveyard or the abandoned wood mill behind the 7-11 and smoke a joint or sneak sips from the booze I stole from my mom's liquor cabinet. We were wise-asses and bored by school and wanted to see how far we could push our luck.

I drove drunk on slick winter roads and passed out in broad daylight in odd places. Tanya was there beside me, looking out for me. Like when I put my mother's orange Vega up on two wheels rounding a corner at 70 mph, and the time I spewed purple Mad Dog on the shoes of my physics teacher, and when I stepped through the ice during one of Jim Campbell's blowouts at his dad's hunting camp on Indian River.

She made me feel scared and alive, like when I raced across the bridge to Mosquito Island as a child. If I'd stopped to think about us or the future, I would be lost and I knew it: skid out over an embankment, drown in icy waters, burn in bed from cigarette flames. We were moths and lamps both, blinking in daylight, dizzy at night. She loved me, she said, and that was almost enough.

Wilderness

Running away. A specialty of mine. Jolene can see the restlessness in my eyes whenever she brings up domestic subjects: children, house, a safe place to live. We've been married less than a year and already I can see that she's at wit's end. I've kept her at arm's length the way I do my friends, coworkers, even my mother who phones every Saturday like clockwork.

But then my mother stopped calling. I didn't worry at first because she doesn't have an answering machine. Then weeks stretched into months. Finally, I called my father's sister Pam who told me that my mother had been admitted to the county hospital after having felt run down the whole summer. I took a leave of absence from my job and grabbed the next plane home.

On the flight, my head was in a thousand places at once. I found myself thinking back to almost ten years before—my 18th birthday party on Mosquito Island. My friends from the hockey team had been there with their groupies, the town's pot dealer came with his contingent, and Tanya and Karen flirted with me good-naturedly and egged me into a drinking binge. I polished off a bottle of JD practically by myself. I was planning on telling Tanya I loved her, but I fell asleep next to the small bonfire we'd made. Tanya was there to catch me, I was told later, before I fell face-first into the flames.

The first thing I did when I landed at the airport, even before I rented a car or found out when visiting hours were at Alpena General Hospital, was to track down Tanya's number from her mother and leave a message on her machine to meet at dusk on Mosquito Island. We had unfinished business and I knew I would need someone to talk to if what I feared was true.

That afternoon was a blur of nurses, specialists, and my mom's maladies: bronchitis, pneumonia, urinary tract infection. My Aunt Pam prayed in the corner of the room and I could barely meet my mother's eyes, who'd aged three years for each year I'd been gone. She squeezed my hand tightly and we looked at the TV above her bed, silently, watching the lips move with the sound turned all the way down.

Finally, Pam excused herself after the evening news. Mom turned to me, her eyes puffy and red. "I'm sorry," she said.

"I know, mom."

"I'll give up smoking, drinking. I'll become a better person."

"The doctor says you're going to have to...if you want to live."

"Would you like that?"

"How can you even ask a thing like that?"

Mom sighed, brushing her brown bangs back from glistening cheeks. "I can see the shame in your eyes even now.

"Mom, I-"

"Shhh," she said, placing her forefinger to my lips.

The nurse returned with a dinner tray. "Visiting hours are over. Your mom's tired."

I stood and watched as the harried RN unwrapped foil from around steaming plastic, unveiling chicken, peas, mashed potatoes, and apple cobbler.

"I'll be back tomorrow," I said

"Son, tell Jolene everything about us. She deserves to know. With her, you have a chance."

I nodded as the nurse whisked by in a swish of cotton, ushering me out the door.

Reunion

I circled Mosquito Island, looking for Tanya. It was more than an hour past dusk and I figured she'd either blown me off or hadn't gotten my message. Night made the once-familiar island unsettling, closing up decades-old walkways and causing unforeseen glades. I couldn't help thinking about what I'd tell my wife when I called her tonight or my mother tomorrow. I felt my way to the tree stump where Tanya and I used to hang out and saw a circle of light flickering in the blackness. From my stint in the Marines, I knew it was a cigarette, having seen many of them glow in the dark while sneaking up on imaginary prey.

"Scott," called out a voice I thought I'd never hear again.

"Hi, Tanya. Glad you could make it."

"Jesus, you scared me to death. Come on over here."

The moon hadn't yet risen. I stumbled over a tree root on my way to the stump where she sat, inhaling and exhaling gray smoke.

I placed my hand on her shoulder to find the narrow berth beside her. "Did you ever notice that I picked the smallest stump on the island so you'd have to brush against me when we stopped here?"

"Quit, already. I was the one who picked the spot. Don't even start. You were the one who turned your back on me. How many letters did I send you when you were in the military, in college?"

"I was crazy about you, you know."

"You sure have a funny way of showing it...how's your mom doing?"

"Not that hot."

"Sorry to hear it."

"I'm not. I mean, I'm glad she didn't pass away all of a sudden like my dad."

"Death is tough. Slow or fast. Ever since you left, it's

been like you were dead…to me…your friends. Even when you came to visit, it was like seeing another person."

I felt her eyes burn through me, hotter than the cigarette, brighter than the unblinking moonrise. Neither of us wanted to talk about the morning after my 18th birthday, when I woke up in the back of Tanya's car while she and Zeke, the hockey team left winger, went at it in the front seat. My clothes were soaking wet from having slipped off the bridge into the duck pond. They were still a bit damp eight hours later when I got off the bus in Detroit at the Marine recruiting station.

"How come you never tried to kiss me?" she asked.

"I couldn't stand the thought of losing you, like my dad, my mom…."

"You haven't lost her yet."

Tanya slipped her hand in mine. We talked about our problems with family, failed relationships, drugs, our penchant for too much booze and too little exercise. We discussed our spouses and discovered we'd married similar people.

The hours passed and the moon poked above the trees, lighting up the faces of teenagers in parked cars beside the duck pond, the distant windows of the hospital, waving evergreen branches and mallards splashing in the pond. The ducks had traveled long distances to be with family and friends. Tanya poked fun at me when I told her this and ran her hands through my pockets for smokes. I pushed her away halfheartedly and stared out at the hospital, the top floors beaming even white teeth.

I was back home with the first love of my life...and it was time for me to rebuild my relationship with her. Not with the woman leaning into my shoulder or my wife who'd already put up with a lifetime of moodiness, but rather the woman who gave me birth. Every man's first love...from which he never truly escapes.

Radio Radio

Floyd commenced his radio show in the dark, announcing his litany of ailments to the ivy reaching down from the roof of the overpass where he lived. He marched out into the pre-dawn dusk and broadcast the weather to the lamp posts, which snapped to attention as he passed. The benches and billboards seemed interested in business updates of yard sales, hot dog vendors, and rewards for missing pets. As he strode confidently along the concrete corridors the auto machines parted for him like the Red Sea had for Moses. Objects knew him for the misunderstood radio celebrity that he was. And yet, somewhere in the black hole of his past, he remembered his broadcast would be impossible without transistors and towers, Marconi men and an atmosphere to bounce his voice from city to city, like his problems, his family, his past.

As Floyd made his way to the Boulevard he watched the earth's own star strip the shadows from Hollywood like varnish from a dusty piece of wood. He quickly moved his show to the Walk of Fame, where he began his "man on the street" interviews. Today, like every day, he saw a different galaxy of faces with cameras looped around their necks and "I Love L.A." T-shirts protecting their bodies. Floyd asked them their names and stuck his microphone under their chins, but they slapped his hand and hurried past, refusing to answer the question of the day. Not quite a fair label, since the question was always the same: "Why doesn't gravity keep things from flying apart?"

After an uninspired meatball sandwich from an alley dumpster behind Musso and Frank's restaurant, he felt the afternoon drag his spirits earthward, his missing life and wife entwined in his gullet, a shrinking quasar burning ever less hotly, growing more dense, a shade of the star it once was, he once was. He was rooted in place seemingly a lifetime, and the only thing that moved him from his stoop was a horn laughing shrilly. He followed the sound to the Boulevard, where he regained reception and his show broke out of commercials.

The dead air settled in his lungs as he fought for words, for meaning, but he couldn't quit. His listeners depended on him, didn't they? He launched wearily into the one o'clock news and his confidence buoyed as the starlight overhead broke through the haze. He reported on potholes the size of satellites that the city refused to fix, shopping carts stolen by police, trash that continued its yearly migration in a circular pattern around the city like the Milky Way.

On one street corner, a German tourist asked him the way to Mann's Chinese Theater and Floyd told him it was on the singing mountain between the moon and sun, where his radio station was, his lost love. Afterwards, he hummed the afternoon music play list and wandered Hollywood Boulevard, where the stars, both named and unnamed, disappeared beneath his feet. Life made more sense like this—with the sky below.

As afternoon gave way to twilight, the sidewalk swelled with tourists and men ducking into bars and XXX bookstores. This meant it was time for the traffic report. He warned the postcard displays in T-shirt shops about the stalled traffic and the accidents that occurred. He reached out to those mired in rush hour, men and women heading home to spouses and children, telling them how a few too many drinks or a bad gamble with the rent or infidelity could wrest them from their lives.

But there was hope, after all, even on the news. He informed the pigeons that it was dinner time at the Golden Harbor retirement home. He stopped to make sure no one had stolen the Styrofoam change container from Wanda, who'd already passed out in the doorway of the condemned building next to Playboy Liquor. And he met up with Samuel, a blind junkie who staked out the 7-Eleven parking lot, and gave him the day's highlights. As he broadcast, Samuel smiled and nodded at the right places. His station had its fans, after all. Radio waves bounced from Hollywood to that realm where visible light, microwaves, and God met to discuss the universe. And him. And whether either had any beginning or end. When he left, Samuel said it was great seeing him.

Floyd felt tired and his throat was raw. He grabbed some dinner at the Hollywood Mission, interviewed some new arrivals at the Greyhound Station, and wandered home past the bus stop beside his overpass. A woman waited for the 8:00 bus as she did every night. She waved at him and he stopped to give her a preview of things to come: high tide and low tide, sunrise and sunset, the date and its astrological significance, and he ended with astronomy.

"Tonight Mars and Saturn will be visible in the sky between the Hollywood sign and the 101 overpass. Several stars may be visible through the night smog. The moon is waning, almost new. We will feel an emptiness in our hearts tonight."

The woman smiled. In broken English, she told him how he reminded her of the man in the "go glass."

"Yes," he said, "I was, am an astronomer."

She pointed at the crosswalk signal as the tiny man in it turned from red to a celestial white. Alone and generic. Unheeded and absolutely necessary. Every day and night, the small white man kept moving his feet, warning and helping, moving from bad to good, future and past, trying to rediscover who he was and what kept things from falling apart.

Summer Snows

There's nothing lonelier than driving at night. Headlights flicker a madman's eyes alongside homes and businesses you can't quite see. The details that hint at humanity no longer exist in the dark and tonight I feel an emptiness no food, drink, or man can hope to fill. I throttle the car until the steering wheel vibrates, accelerating to the bumpers of other cars before shooting past. If I were the other drivers, I would hate me, too.

I learned to drive in a cemetery. My father told me it was convenient in case of a fatal accident. Dad rarely jokes and when he does it's almost never about death. Maybe it was the pressure of returning to White Pines Cemetery after so many years, forcing himself to make light of the countless hours we'd spent around Ken's tombstone.

The first year after my brother died in the crib, we

were there almost every weekend. It became our family's church. Finally, my father broke down, telling my mother "No, WE'RE not going today." But she wouldn't let go. Even now I know she still hangs out at his tombstone. I'm surprised we haven't crossed paths. I go there myself…and grieve in a way…but for different reasons.

The crackle of tires on roadside gravel snaps me back to the task at hand as I hurtle along I-94 from the University of Michigan where I spent the night partying with friends. I dread going back to my parents' house. It's late July and I've been bored for weeks in the suburban Detroit strip mall I grew up in. The party didn't do much to cheer me, although I managed to get blitzo. The usual culprits were involved: beer, pot, pills—one blue, one purple—a couple shots of tequila. I started getting tired of the guys hitting on me until my roommate from freshman year Leslie winked conspiratorially and handed me a white nasal spray. I took three blasts in each nostril and sneezed my head off, but I've been wired ever since. Wired and sluggish both.

At moments like this I pretend I'm back in White Pines learning to drive, nothing to hit but concrete and trees, no one to smash into…living that is. Even now, Dad's voice reassures me, "Elizabeth, if ever you worry about where your car is, look to the edge of the hood and that's where your tires are on the road." I try to ignore the blinding beams across the divider.

It's a bad time to be getting back. Most of the bars will be closing soon and it'll be hard to track down my homies and find out where the parties are. My boyfriend of the moment, "Mr. Right Now," I call him, went on a border run to Ontario to seedy Canadian bars where he and his pals can drink. Probably a titty bar. I won't be able to sleep for several hours at least. Plenty of time to get in trouble. The road ahead swims with ghostly headlights of others searching for home.

******* ******* *******

I wake at noon, if you can call it waking, since I hadn't slept a wink. I closed my eyes around sunrise and let a kaleidoscope of thoughts and colors wash over my mind, which churned like a washer on continual spin. I turn onto my side and my hand glides over Vic's pale torso into wisps of red chest hair. Light streams through curtainless windows onto the foot of his futon. Last night I knew he'd let me in. Vic's always been there for me, even when I'm a bitch-on-wheels.

Others see him differently. In high school, his name was Crazy Vic, crazy for carrying a plastic leprechaun in his pocket, crazy for laughing at math problems from the back row, crazy for staying awake for days at a stretch. Everyone thought he was on drugs, but he may be the only person I know who avoided them. Not just the harsh-sounding ones like pot, coke, hash and speed, but also the exotic varieties our parents gobble—Valium, Percodan, Halcion and Viagra—drugs that sound like minor Greek Gods or thousand-dollar-a-day vacation destinations.

Vic lifts his head and brushes the tip of my nose as though swatting off an alarm. He glances at his bedside clock and collapses beside me.

"Christ, you kept me up late. Forgot to set it."

"What's with the clock? Turning over a new leaf?"

"If I was, I wouldn't stoop to doing your boyfriend's dirty work."

"Cute," I say, unwilling to let him off the hook. "Why do you need an alarm?"

"A research job at the University. Pays thirty dollars."

"For you, that must be mad money for a month."

"Not so cute," he says.

After his dad died, something in Vic snapped. He dropped out of school and quickly set about destroying his life. He sponged off his mom for a while, then began selling his stamp, baseball card, and comic book collections. He was down to silver dollars now and the remains of his 60s Barbie Doll collectibles. That and a few odd jobs: yard work in summer, shoveling snow in winter, test subject for psychology students at the University of Michigan.

"You look like hell, Liz. You need to start taking care of yourself. Remember your friends: sleep and food? Well, they don't remember you."

"I can get this kind of abuse at home."

"No," he says, rubbing his unshaven face. "You get different abuse there. Why don't you come to breakfast with me?"

"Sorry." I say, rising. "I've got things to do. Can't slow down."

"Never could."

I search for discarded clothing and try to stay mad at him for sticking his shnoz in my business, but by the time I button my red velvet dress and slip on my combat boots, I have a hard time not jumping in bed with him and wasting the day away.

"Change your mind?"

"Go to hell," I say with a smile, stepping over a pile of used appliances and castoffs from his dumpster diving on my way to the door.

******* ******* *******

Outside Vic's apartment, I hurry past a couple of skateboard kids who look like they can get their hands on anything in the spectrum of the alphabet—from AK-47s to PCP to stolen VCRs. I jump into my father's beat-up BMW for the ten-minute haul back to Key Lake Subdivision. I can't help wondering what Darren would do if he found out about my cheating. I don't have an excuse, except my affection for Vic is genuine. We dated off and on in high school, and were even sweethearts back in the fourth grade when we lived on the same downtown block before urban professionals left the Motor City in droves. The city reminds me of my family, uneasy in the daytime, haunted at night.

I punch the accelerator and go screaming at 75 mph past Key Lake College, where Dad teaches English. Calvin Klein's army marches across the tiny campus, taking summer classes and checking themselves for conformity. I'm wiped and don't relish the explanations I'll have to make at home for staying out all night. The whole drive back, I've got the creeps like someone is following me. I get that paranoid feeling sometimes at school, when I get hopped up and stroll campus sidewalks from party to party, chatty girlfriends in tow.

Thankfully, my parents' cars are gone when I get home. I walk into the cluttered two floor Victorian, remodeled last year and refitted with aluminum siding as though the armor would protect us from the dark cloud hovering above our house. I stop in the kitchen, suddenly dizzy. My insides feel lighter than air. I can't remember the last time I ate. I start mixing myself a diet shake. Chocolate. 180 calories. I check my message board on the fridge, where there's an initialed note from my mother.

Elizabeth,

Please be ready at 9 p.m. for your father. Tonight is the premiere of Nate Thompson's film Spykiller. Since he is a good writing connection, you should make it a point to attend. Try to wear something appropriate.

JM

No, it can't ever be a friendly note signed Love Mom or Love Dad, but always a pressure-filled memo with a JM, DM, or my own EM. Christ, why can't they remember I write poetry, POETRY. Don't they listen to a damn thing I say?

At least I can take comfort in the fact that my parents are more messed up than I am. They don't talk to each other unless absolutely necessary. Dad drowns himself in academia and food—last week I saw the king of binge eaters swill a bottle of barbecue sauce from the fridge. Mom works part time, goes horseback riding three times a week, and fixes up the attic (her sun room) with continual remodeling and used appliances. But a second stove? In the attic? No one—friends, family or independent contractors—can figure that one out. I wonder if Dad has raised his insurance premiums because of it and if Mom will soon be needing another "trip to the country": the code my parents use when discussing her visits to a private institution.

I hear a rustling in the doorway and wonder if it's my no-good bro William home from baseball practice, video games, or whatever he does these days to avoid the home front. I stick my head out in the hallway and I'm met by moist lips and the bristle of a blond goatee. I can't help laughing and diet shake dribbles from my nostrils.

Darren shakes his head. "Gross."

"I thought nothing grossed you out," I say, not sure whether I'm happy to see my boyfriend or if I should chew him out for walking in without knocking. "Christ, you almost made me scream."

"Quit bitching. You like surprises," Darren says with a sneer that makes his 6'4" frame seem even more taut and wiry. He has a manic gleam in his eyes—a look I know means trouble, like when he got the idea to link our nipple rings together during sex and one of his metal rings ripped out, staining the carpeting with blood as I ushered him to the emergency room in the middle of the night. My parents bought my excuse later of a nosebleed... or pretended they did.

"So where are the dumbatic duo?" Darren asks, as though reading my mind.

"Out," I say, feeling exhausted and jonesing for a warm bath and cool sheets to slide into.

"Looks like you've been out all night."

"I could say the same about you."

"We might as well keep partying."

"Not a good idea, but still...I can always sleep tomorrow. What's the plan?"

He reaches out and takes my hand, leading me toward the door. "It's a surprise."

****** ****** ******

Surprise.

Darren uses the word like a kid uses sugar on cereal, sneaking another spoonful at every opportunity, never getting tired of "too much of a good thing."

As bad as I look after a day and a half without sleep, Darren looks three times worse, and probably has been up three times as long.

"Hear footsteps outside?" I ask.

"Don't get paranoid. I cleared everything," Darren says.

It feels as though the walls of the musty stone mausoleum are closing around the four of us hiding inside. Cindy and Morton stop talking and shoot me uneasy looks. We aren't used to staring at one another in daylight, even the poor variety streaming through the window grating. Usually, we sneak over to White Pines Cemetery at midnight or later, when the only illumination sparks from matchbooks or the white fire dancing inside our minds.

"What do you mean, clear it? With Randy?"

"Yeah, with Randy."

"He was a fuck-up, even in high school."

"You almost done with that?" Cindy asks, eyebrows rising above a pair of gas station sunglasses, a dribble of clear fluid leaking from her right nostril.

Darren rocks the edge of a razor over the jagged white

flecks he'd dumped onto the stone coffin. "Cool your jets, girl. My sinuses are messed up. The last batch felt like ground glass."

There's nothing more pathetic than speed freaks waiting for their high. Nervous laughter and nervous chatter bounce off the walls, almost as though if we keep talking we'll respark the fire that makes us think we can solve the world's ills, or at least reorganize our coat closets.

Cindy paces madly from one end of Darren's grandparents' crypt to the other, her hands deep in her hip-hugging jeans as she hums "Singing in the Rain." Morton fidgets on a stenciled angel in the stairwell, tying and retying his shoelaces in an intricate loop. Darren rests his elbows on his grandmother's coffin lid, scooping, piling, chopping, and dividing lines of crank.

We've already blazed through a crapload of Darren's stash, and although he's generous with his merchandise, you can see the machine whir in the blacks of his pupils, computing how much meth to use and what to keep for later—until his next batch arrives. He stretches four long lines on the stone lid.

"Dinner's ready," Darren calls in a singsong voice. It's a tired joke and we know it. All it does is remind me of dinner later that evening with the folks, the one family function they insist I show up for.

Each in turn, we bend down over Darren's grandmother, licking our chapped lips and snorting lines and wiping away tears from stinging noses and slugging back the now-warm sports drink Morton swiped from the Easy-Mart.

The others launch into a conversation about lame Detroit radio stations and smoke cigarettes. I throw in an occasional word or two, but mostly I'm angry. I don't know if it's because I'm chain-smoking even though I told myself I'd quit, or inhaling drugs I promised I'd take only on Friday nights, or maybe it's listening to Darren's sarcastic laughter, which has begun grating on my nerves. Things have not been the same between us since the week he and I spent in my dorm room during spring break. My roommate was gone and my parents bought my excuse of staying at school to complete a term paper. We stayed awake the whole week, snorting the mammoth stock of crystal meth he hadn't sold finals week and knocking ourselves out with marathon sex.

Toward the end we were drained from lack of food and sleep, but couldn't stop helping ourselves to his stash. The last few nights we sat in the almost-empty dorm, talked-out, sniffling and light-headed, listening to the March winds whistle through the window cracked for our endless stream of cigarette smoke. The walls creaked and my roommates' poster of Lady Gaga wavered and her mouth seemed to move. We both began experiencing full-form apparitions. Mine were of my family as they would be in death, haunting me for letting them down. His were of teenage ODs, blaming him for getting me and so many others hooked. I begged for him to hold me as I stuffed my ears with cotton, closed my eyes, and prayed for sleep to carry me away, but he couldn't stand it. His ghosts and my cries for help sent him bolting to his car and speeding back to Bloomfield Hills. He jokes about it now. I do not.

"Shit," I say.

"What's up?" Darren sniffs loudly and wipes his nose with the back of his hand.

"I left my extra pack of cigarettes in your car, I'll be back in a sec."

It's a lie, but I don't care. I rush toward the bottom of the steps where Morton is fumbling inside the cargo pocket of his cut-off khakis. "I've got some extras."

"No, I need filtered. I'll see you guys in a few, OK?"

Darren shrugs his shoulders. "Suit yourself."

I climb the stairs and slip out the iron-wrought door, not caring if the White Pines staff sees me as I hurry to the nearby back fence and a hole in the chain link. As I duck out of the cemetery I see my mother driving slowly in front of the entrance as though contemplating a quick dash inside, but instead she steps on the gas at the end of the block and blows past the stop sign with a screeching right turn. Where's Dad, anyway? Saturdays are supposed to be his day to watch her.

Dad and I are both used to running away from our problems, I guess. Like I'm doing now with Darren. My folks aren't exactly the best role models in the love department, though. They met in college, pinned each other with Greek symbols, and rushed into marriage. I doubt either one of them's ever slept with another person. Once when I was fourteen, Mom burst out with a graphic description of the birds and bees, and her fear of being crushed in bed by a wheezing, hairy fat man.

A white pick-up shoots past me, blaring its horns, the guy inside screaming for me to get out of the way. Somehow, I've wandered out into the middle of the street. The summer breeze dances along my skin glistening with sweat. I didn't notice it before, but it's actually a pretty day to walk the two-mile trek home. White clouds stroll along rooftops without a care in the world.

And there is nothing, absolutely nothing, inside of me.

****** ****** ******

Dinner is served at six on the dot as always. My brother William makes a cameo halfway through, Dad shares anecdotes about his students as he wolfs pot roast and Mom makes less sense than usual, discussing meal after meal after meal from her childhood growing up on a farm in South Central Illinois. We feign politeness so we can pretend, for a half hour at least, we have a typical American family. I haven't heard William speak for weeks and my parents punctuate fifteen years of separate beds with forced smiles. And each dinner, we teeter on the verge of spitting out our spiciest secrets, our kettle of fears, our tastiest addictions, which remain just on the tip of our tongues, before being swallowed inside.

I'm still riding high on the meth, but I manage to force down all the vegetables on my plate and a bite or two of overcooked beef. They don't ask where I was the night before.

Afterwards, I follow Mom into the kitchen. We have a routine—I rinse the dishes in the sink and she loads them into the dishwasher.

"So why were you at cemetery today?" Mom asks, spinning a plate into the plastic rack.

"It's funny, I was going to ask you the same thing. It's not healthy, Mom, going there that often."

"At least I don't want to end up there permanently," she says, closing the dishwasher door and pushing the cleaning jets in motion.

"What are you saying...I want to die?"

"Everyone around here thinks I'm stupid, but I see what's going on."

"And what's going on?"

"You think you have an absentee mother, don't you? But I'm here. You know? I'm here!"

"Where else would you be?"

"With him. With Ken. I know everyone blames me for his death."

"Mom, I–"

"You grow up so quickly," she says wistfully, her panic subsiding. "Your father doesn't understand this, but I know you and William have already left me. You're dead to me. Spirits." With that, she turns on her heels back up to her attic room, leaving my mouth gaping with "I'm sorry" still unsaid.

****** ****** ******

An hour later I try to pull myself together in my room, playing music and attempting to ease the day and drugs out of my system. The shower I took helps a bit, but my relaxation is jolted by a knock on the door. I get up from bed and throw on a robe to answer it.

"What is it?"

The door opens, sending me backpedaling. Two wiry arms pick me up and slam me onto my mattress.

"Darren, cut it out. I'm not in the mood."

We wrestle for a while. When he sees I won't give in, he rolls off in a huff. "Man, I don't believe it. Is everything psycho today? This is a first, YOU turning down sex."

"Get out. I'm already on thin ice with my folks."

"You mean you're on thin ice with me," he says, rubbing his knuckles, which are cracked and bruised.

"What are you talking about?"

"You think I'm stupid, don't you?"

"I don't know. Tell me how you messed up your hand, then I'll let you know."

"You think you're so smart. Sneaking around on your folks, getting away with murder. Well, I'm not your parents."

I look into Darren's eyes and see nothing but a wall of air.

"Go home and get some sleep. Come back when you're sober."

He clenches his teeth and grabs my wrist. "I've been following you when you visit that old boyfriend of yours—Crazy Vic, isn't it? When you split on me today I paid him a visit." He rubs his fist and gives me a smile. "He'll think twice before getting between us again."

I reach into my bedside bureau and grab an open bag of speed I keep for emergencies. I toss the white flakes in his face. "This is what's getting between us, Darren."

"You crazy, ungrateful bitch."

I don't think, just strike forward with my knee into his groin. Darren woofs as he collapses fetal on the floor.

"Listen, if you hurt Vic, I'm going to make sure you're locked up. I don't want to see you around here again. Got it?"

I can tell he understands by his groan of agreement as I hurry out the door with a handful of clothes. "It was one punch, Liz," he cries after me. "It's your fault, you know?"

******* ******* *******

Darren's right, in his own messed-up way. I should have told him the truth, but I've never been good at shaking a bad habit. I cruise the near desolate streets of East Birmingham searching for Vic. His flat is empty, his door swung open into the second floor hallway. I fear the worst. Vic doesn't handle adversity well. I remember when Greg Stevens tripped him in the grade school lunchroom, making him spill pea soup on his pants and shoes. He cocked his fist, marched to the nearest wall, and broke four fingers pummeling the brick schoolhouse. Whenever I hold his hand, I can still feel the protruding ridges.

Vic and I are bound by our fascination with death as much as anything. I first got to know him by using him as an actor in a series of 8 mm films. Most of them involved the family pets, Vic as a mass murderer, and buckets of fake blood made from my own concoction of light Karo syrup, salt, and red dye #5. My favorite starring role for him was as the enigmatic super hero do-gooder Captain ?, who concealed the answer to any cosmic emergency beneath his red satin bathrobe. He seemed indestructible then.

I drive past Howell Park, Vic's favorite haunt, scanning the regulars in the blossoming dusk. The picnic tables by the duck pond are empty. A tattered blanket drifts along gouged sod. A familiar silhouette shivers beside a white-haired black man on a park bench sucking at a cigarette butt that isn't lit. I pull over to the curb and rush out of the car, engine still running.

"Those skyscrapers are really alive. They got teeth. You won't catch me going anywhere near those suckers. If you don't heed Teddy's words, they're gonna bend down and suck you in. Ain't that right, Teddy?" the old man asks half to himself, half to Vic. An empty fifth of Jim Beam rolls off the graffitied bench and clatters on the sidewalk. "You listening to me, boy? It looks like one of 'em beat up on you pretty good already."

I run up to Vic and wrap my arms around him, separating him from his drinking buddy. I shake him, gently at first, then slap his puffy face. He comes to with a start, reeling off the bench into a trash barrel.

"Auntie Em. Auntie Em. Take me home," Vic says, struggling to regain his balance.

"Better watch him, miss. The buildings, they been gnawing on his soul like an old soup bone. You should hear the nonsense he's been talking about flying monkeys, speed demons, and the devil his self."

"Liz?" Vic sinks his face into my breasts, his breath

reeking of whiskey. "Is that you?" He drops to his knees in broken glass and yellowing paper.

"Yes. It's me."

"You don't hate me?"

"No."

"Then you love me?"

I open my mouth, but no words came out.

"Then you love me? Huh?"

"Vic, you're drunk. You don't know what you're saying."

I drag him to the car, help him into the back seat and drive him home. My home. I'll be damned if I'm going to let him spend the night alone. He looks like hell, his face plastered with tears, mud, and blood. I help him through the garage, up the back staircase, and into my bed before anyone is the wiser. Thank god Darren had enough sense to split.

I slip off Vic's clothes, brush the powder off my sheets and tuck him in. Damn. It's already 8:55. Dad will be breaking away any moment from his keyboard where he is writing a million page thesis on whether the ingredients in the witch's cauldron in MacBeth formed a hallucinogenic drug. Like father, like daughter, I guess. I barely have time to wiggle into a plain black dress and high heels before I hear his tentative rapping.

"Just a sec, Dad. I gotta throw on lipstick."

"Hurry up, Elizabeth. I'm going to start the car."

****** ****** ******

"Maybe you should buckle up, Liz."

"Maybe you should slow down, Dad."

"Elizabeth Martin, NOW."

"OK, don't have a cow."

I reach for my belt as we careen at high speeds past suburban strip malls and gated subdivisions. I forgot how aggressive Dad gets behind the wheel. I haven't been in a car with him since he taught me the rules of the road. We don't speak much the first half of the trip, and I find myself worrying about Vic and hoping Mom won't pick tonight to leaf through my diary or rifle my underwear drawer for joints. When Dad opens his mouth, he tells the story (for the umpteenth time) about how his high school buddy Nate Thompson became one of the hottest screenwriters in the country.

The story's long and filled with bleak moments that turn to success with faith and old-fashioned elbow grease. Before I know it, we're pulling up to a cobblestone driveway filled with BMWs and Mercedes, instead of the limousines I was expecting. Nate meets us at the door in a funky robe Dad tells me is a smoking jacket. A balcony sweeps from the landing into a wide, circular stairway. Waiters in white tuxes serve odd-looking snacks and the house stretches forever in all directions. As impressive as this guy's place is, I'm disappointed none of the movie's stars have made it to the premiere. In fact, it seems no one has shown up who didn't play for the Sterling Trojans High School football team when Nate was starting quarterback.

The whole scene is pathetic, like being in the middle of a bad high school reunion. Even the screening of the hundred million dollar movie can't hold my interest. Being a good flirt isn't even enough to keep the film's seductress from being pumped full of lead. And I'm starting to crash without a fix, my legs wobbly, my head spinning from the drinks I'm sneaking.

After the screening, the impossible happens. It gets worse. Howling men with bulging faces and bulging bellies start reliving every play of their championship season. I'm mortified as I watch my Dad hike a couch pillow through his legs to Touchdown Nate Thompson who makes the other aging ex-high-school athletes run into the billiard room for the long passes. The wives stand on the side like cheerleaders. Their plastered smiles help me understand what drives my mother to talk to herself and bake cookies in a converted attic. I attempt to drink a Long Island Ice Tea from every bar in the place, an even dozen altogether. I flirt with one of the bartenders and decide that I will never-ever attend a high school reunion.

By the time dad tracks me down, I've made it a point

to vomit in every bathroom I can find and even a few rooms with white tiles I think might later be converted into bathrooms. It's a quiet ride home that becomes even quieter after the old man veers off the highway to spread pot roast like tar onto the shoulder of the road. When he gets back in, I turn to him and say, "Why did you leave me alone back there?"

"I didn't see you," he says.

"You and mom both. She said earlier I was a ghost."

"You're certainly skinny enough," he says angrily, jamming the car in drive. "You wanna tell me what your real problem is?"

"Life!" I spit out, with as much spite as I can manage.

Dad's eyes turn from angry to downcast as he stares along the side of the car as it knifes through the highway. Finally, he clears his throat and mutters, "Jesus, what am I supposed to do? No one's more invisible in our god-damn family than me."

******* ******* *******

The next morning I wake from a dream where I'm struggling through a snowdrift, pushing through endless cascades of powder toward a distant light that becomes a country house with a lawn of green grass and flower petals poking through the carpet of snow. I'm hungry and more than a little hungover. It's already past eleven. Vic moans beside me, in the middle of his own dream, fingers knotted in the sheets. His black eye has purpled in the night like wild posies bursting into bloom and I'm not sure what I'll say when he gets up.

For once, I want to be there for him, but I wonder how much good I'll be. I can't take care of myself or the family falling apart around me. And yet, despite how shitty yesterday was, the emptiness inside me seems smaller. Most days I worry the nothingness will expand beneath my skin until it turns me inside out and I disappear altogether.

I stagger to my feet and open the shades. My father is standing outside my window in the rose bushes. He looks up, noticing me, his mouth filled to bursting, a block of cheddar cheese half-eaten in his hands. There goes his diet again, I think, wondering if Mom is up in the attic and if she'll mind me going up to visit her today. Although unclothed, I don't bother covering myself. I'm not invisible, a ghost, and neither is Dad, caught on the other side of the looking glass from me, a victim of grief as much as Mom, as much as me.

Finally, he tilts his head and checks out Vic stirring in bed beside me. He shakes his head. So do I. We stand for a good long while, staring at each other through the sun-streaked glass, our secrets exposed like a patch of bad road, relief on both our faces for what we can no longer ignore.

The Dancing Interrogator

The interrogator in retirement was drawn to a place where he would not feel compelled to dig for answers. He moved to a neighborhood in Los Angeles with signs in three languages, none of which he understood. He did not need island vistas and umbrella drinks, or the kind of women that were drawn to such things. He craved mystery and bustle that he could not comprehend or control.

Some days he was not entirely certain what he was eating and made sure to move often so that his mail would not catch up to him. His friends were all dissectors, and he did not relish his last days as a lab frog beneath the gaze of helpful vivisectionists.

As his own body began to fail him bit by bit, he became interested in the truth of flesh, not sexual gratification, but something bordering on intuition, the way animals smell out friendship and danger. He signed up for a dance class and was a quick study, used to the mimicry of others in pursuit of his former craft. His instructors doted on him and his creaky knees through the samba, ballroom twirls, and soft-shoe tap. He stayed in rhythm no matter what was thrown at him: calypso, jitterbug, the moonwalk.

Women jockeyed to be his partner, all but the Latin-Afro-Asian beauty who stomped on his toes on their only tango, perhaps blinded by the curtain of curly bangs. He was assigned to her, of course, to see if he could help work out the kinks in her style.

He might as well have danced with the moon. He stumbled and pitched to a strange gravitational pull, toward the floor and alternately her breasts. He apologized, was slapped, was winked at, was confused by divergent signals.

Still, she agreed to go out with him after their final class. He wondered if he was the only man who did not want a name, an origin or surname, a story that would lead to familiarity, longing, and sorrow. He stared into an elixir that he asked the bartender to serve without divulging its contents and readied himself to dance his way among theirs pasts, prepared to follow, to lead, to grab sore feet, to fall as one figure into the future.

Vegas Everywhere I Go

How was I supposed to know? I hear footsteps in the room above me and the old man's already at work. Right? His car is gone and when I leave my pad I see a shadow moving inside his place. So I walk down the street to the Howling Dog Saloon and call the cops. Then I chill out in the backyard of the shitty apartment complex my dad owns and knock back a can of Coke to wake up. Still got a bit of a hangover from last night. The local 5-0 shows with their rollers spewing red and blue, but no siren. They get out and I tell 'em about the prowler. These crackers get a wicked gleam in their eyes, whip their guns out, and creep up the stairs.

The cops pound on the door, but there's no response. Luckily, it's unlatched. A lot of these country fucks leave their doors unlocked, although dad says hooligans like me are changing that. Anyway, the pigs check out the place until the only room left is the old man's bedroom. The pudgy cop, barely older 'n me, puts a finger up to his mouth and pulls a coat hanger outta the front closet. The son'bitch hands me his piece and starts to pick the shabby lock. My hand shakes...with excitement! Maybe these crackers aren't so bad after all.

The guy's ancient partner frowns at me and whispers, "It ain't loaded. Only loaded pistol we allow in this town is mine." He looks at me all serious, like I'm gonna mess with him.

The lock clicks and the fat cop almost tumbles face first into the room. I look around the corner and see my old man throwing a blanket over someone. Dad looks none too pleased about the older cop's handgun aimed at his face. "Could you please point that somewhere else," he says coolly, although he's got to be scared. Shitless. He looks at me peeking around the corner and he gestures with his eyes toward the cops like I'm supposed to do something, so I say, "Oh, no, that's not a thief, that's my dad. He lives here."

Both cops look disappointed and apologize. My dad mutters something about having left his car at a bar and calling in sick to work. I blurt out, "Whoops," and backpedal away. The lump under his bedding doesn't say nothing.

"I'll talk to you later," dad promises, shutting the door.

I wonder who he's got stashed under his sheets—if it's a married woman or jailbait. The rumor around town is he's got an appetite for both. Last week when I snuck into his apartment to snag a few beers, I looked in his bedroom closet and found a neck brace on a shelf next to a bull-whip. "A real ladies man," that's how everyone in Belson describes dad. When they aren't giving him shit, that is.

Struggling not to laugh, I get the hell out of dad's love nest. The cops trail behind me and almost get back in their squad car before chubby-wubby remembers he gave me his gun. Damn shame. It'd be nice to have a piece. They wave as they back out of the driveway and tell me not to get into any more trouble. I wave back and start heading toward the bar even though I'm only nineteen.

******* ******* *******

Just what I need, more bullshit I'm gonna get blamed for. As if my problems with my mom's husband Bert ain't already enough. I didn't mean to hit him, just scare him a little. Besides, it wasn't entirely my fault—I was pro-voked—although talking to mom you'd think I was Satan himself. So until things cool down, I decided to come see my dad in bum-fuck, Georgia.

Howling Dog's already half-full, even though it's barely past noon. I order a tequila and OJ, and Mike the bartender says, "'Kay, Joe." My dad, although a Republican dickhead who works as a real estate broker or some such bullshit, set me up good here. He told the owner I was twenty-two and just outta school. The last part is true, but he made it seem like I graduated instead of dropping out of Boise State University near where my mom lives.

Man, I sure don't wanna go back to the apartment complex, not with the old man spitting vinegar, so I look around to see if there's anyone to raise hell with. Only guy I recognize is Vegas (I don't think that's the name his momma gave him) and he grunts in my general direction. I grunt back. I don't like Vegas all that much, although the women sure seem to dig blondilocks. In fact, I think I would have scored here a couple of times if it wasn't for that "between-assignments" construction worker. Still, I try to be nice to him because he's my only pot connection, and since I'm staying the summer with the old man, I have unusually high marijuana needs.

Matter-of-fact, I'm getting kinda short. I supplied one of the deadbeats (as dad calls his renters) with a few joints yesterday so she could go see a movie at the miniplex in town. Her name's Jill and she's kinda cute in a twice-divorced kind of way. I walk over to Vegas who's swirling the cue ball from the pool table in his tanned fingers. He grins at me like the shit-eater he is. "Hey Joey."

"Name's Joe," I say unconvincing-like, knowing it won't do any good, but it's better not to let the dickhead think he can push me around.

"OK, GI fucking Joe. What's shaking, beside yourself?"

"I'm steady as a rock now that I got a drink."

"Probably a virgin."

"Fuck off."

"I was talking about the drink."

"It's a double," I say, although it isn't. Vegas looks at me with a ripsaw grin that makes the people around us probably think we're best buddies giving each other hell. Truth is, we're enemies. Had been from the moment we met. He knows it. I know it. It happens to guys quite often. Making enemies. And you can't always explain why. Maybe it's because he's head rooster around here, although I think it's lame that we're after the same chicks with him being thirty-five and all. As if my dad isn't competition enough.

He sizes me up. "So you're dry, huh?"

"Damn near."

"Let's go get stroked by magic Wanda."

Lame pun. Wanda's the name of his pot connection and, although I've never met her, she's by far my favorite person in Belson.

"Why not. Let's book."

******* ******* *******

Neil Salmon, a.k.a. Slobber. That's who Vegas reminds me of. Slobber was my Junior High School nemesis, especially in gym class. At the time, he was thirteen but looked

156

twenty. I was thirteen and would hit puberty two years later than most of the other guys. There was nowhere to hide that fact in the vicious world of mandatory gym.

I swear to God they should just cage boys from eleven to fifteen.

At first, Slobber seemed content to terrorize me ONLY in the locker room. That was before I made THE mistake. See, one week we were given second-rate weight machines and told to pump iron. While watching one of his pals using the over-the-head-lift apparatus or the jerk machine (as we less muscular types called it), Slobber got his nuts crushed between two twenty-pound weights. He toppled over and the whole gym was silent. Silent except for me. I laughed my ass off and the other boys followed my example. All the while Slobber held his nuts and stared at me with a look of pure rage.

That afternoon, after school, he kicked my ass. The first of many ass-kickings to follow.

******* ******* *******

Vegas and I take my dad's car, mostly because I wanna get it out the parking lot before he gets up and starts yelling at me. We drive along Jackson Street to the south side of town, just past the Quickie Mart. We pass over the 8th Street Bridge where a dozen or so old geezers are out in hip boots and waders in Devil's River. No one's been able to tell me why they'd want to catch fish in that nasty-smelling brown stream. Dad took me fishing out there a couple of times for catfish in his pontoon, but we ended up fighting. As usual. I think he hates me.

We turn at Elmo's Bait and Tackle, and swerve so as not to run over a golden retriever lying dead in the street, tongue hanging out, blood tattooing the asphalt.

"Why'd you bother?" I ask.

"No one deserves to die like that," Vegas says, staring straight ahead, like he's seen a ghost.

I don't have nothing to say to bullshit like that.

Finally, we make our way to the front of a white two-story house—it seems like practically every house in this god-damn town's white—and get out of the car. There's a tickle in the front of my head telling me I'm gonna get a headache soon unless I start drinking again. It's a pain-in-the-ass to start swilling 'em down this early in the day. Oh well. I lean against the hood and hand Vegas three Andrew Jacksons. I'm surprised when he motions for me to follow him. Maybe he figures it's less conspicuous for me to come in than hang out in the yard.

He taps on a ratty screen door and tucks in his shirt like he's going to visit the minister's wife. No answer though. He rips open the screen and his eyes sweep the neighboring yard like a cat. He rears back and gives the front door a hell of a kick. I look down and see filthy white paint flaking off a foot up from the brown welcome mat. The door swings open, followed by a woman's surly voice, "God-damn asshole, you scared the shit out of me."

"Woke you up, you mean." Vegas slips into the house with me at his heels. I see some mean-looking red fingernails clutching the door as it swings shut behind me. Attached to those claws is a five-foot blonde, a little overweight with nice curves. She looks close to forty and with a little makeup could probably pass for thirty. She waves us toward a couch that is covered in dirty clothes, candy wrappers, and old issues of TV Guide. She digs into her purse, pulls out an empty pack of cigarettes, crushes it, and lights a long butt out of a ceramic Virgin Mary ash tray. "Who's the kid, Vegas?"

"Joe...good to meet ya'."

"At least you didn't call me ma'am, there's one in your favor,"

"Yes ma'am." I expect a laugh and get nothing in return but the static from a black-and-white TV getting shitty reception.

"You packing?" Vegas asks.

Wanda shakes her head. "I wish. Should get hooked up tomorrow morning though. Carl's down in Savannah...at the mother lode."

Vegas chuckles and I look around the living room. There's a wooden Pabst Blue Ribbon on Tap sign above the doorway to the kitchen, half-chewed dog toys littering the floor, and several pictures on the wall of a guy I know from The Howling Dog. Carl something or another. He's Vegas' best friend and, apparently, Wanda's guy.

"What you up to today?"

"Baby-sitting." Vegas nudges his elbow into my ribs and smirks.

Wanda smiles and I think about getting the hell outta there. Only the fear of being rude and fucking up my pot connection keeps me sitting in that smoke-filled pigsty. Hanging out with Vegas is always more trouble than it's worth. Last time I saw him, he invited his pal Carl (a dead ringer for Mick Jagger) over to my pad. They ended up drinking all my beer and walking off with Python, my four-foot water pipe. I knew they'd deny taking it if I mentioned it, so I had to start poking holes in beer cans to get high. The next day I sent a couple texts telling the guys back home that Mick Jagger stole my bong.

"Well, the air conditioner's on the fritz and I'm bored."

"Yep, gonna be a scorcher."

"Yep," I add, dreading the options: TV, a matinee repeat, pontooning, the bar.

"Nice day for a swim," Vegas says.

"Sorry my pool's being repaired."

I look around the corner to the backyard but Vegas's snort clues me in that she's just kidding.

"What about the quarry?" Vegas asks.

"Not a bad idea. I haven't been out there yet this summer." Wanda stretches her arms above her head and I make out a tiny sun tattoo on her left breast next to unshaven underarm hair. "The quarry sounds pretty damn good."

They laugh like they're in on some private joke.

"The quarry?"

Vegas looks at me like I'm a cool drink and he's the straw. "Yeah, you up for it, Joey?"

"Sure, why the hell not."

******* ******* *******

We're halfway through one of our three twelve packs before we even get to the swimming hole. I'm sweating in the passenger seat from the heat and sucking air out of the rolled-down window of dad's Plymouth. Vegas is driving (he insisted on it) and cranking The Allman Brothers on the only rock station for a hundred miles. The signal's at least half static and I almost scream at the asshole to turn it off. He's already gotten us lost on dirt roads twice and had to wake up Wanda in the back for directions. She slit her eyes and mumbled something that sounded like Vulcan, and Vegas swore like the drunken good ol' boy he is and jacked the car in reverse. Even now, asleep, Wanda looks pretty ragged out, like she hasn't had a good night's sleep since Kurt Cobain died.

I'm about to pop the top on my fourth beer when we finally ease to a stop next to a chain-link fence behind an Oldsmobile Cutlass. Vegas hoots, "Fucking here," and scratches his belly. We wake up Wanda, haul the beer out of the back seat, and stagger through a hole in the fence toward a swimming hole no bigger than Black Bear Pond back home. The water's clear as hell, the rocks white as bone.

"Used to be a marble quarry, but they hit water from an underground cave. It was the damnedest thing." Vegas tromps through knee-high grass toward an inlet to the water.

Wanda nods. "My dad worked there awhile. The marble they got out of there, they used for tombstones."

"Ain't that a hoot?" Vegas shotguns a beer and starts peeling off his shirt, revealing a broad white chest and biceps striped with farmer's tan.

"The Fish and Wildlife service filled it with perch, but the locals drained the place dry years ago." Wanda lies back on a smooth marble boulder and shields her eyes from the sun. "I ain't up to swimming, but you boys knock yourself out."

******* ******* *******

My folks met years back in the post office here in Belson. My old man just got promoted to Postmaster General, the youngest one ever, he's fond of telling me. At the time, my mom was married to another postal worker, Paul Lyons, who she left for my dad. Local legend has it that my old man stole Paul's woman, fired him, AND kicked his ass to boot. The golden hours of a relationship from hell.

The shit my parents accuse each other of gets wilder by the year. Mom says dad whipped her and my older sister who was fathered by the other postal worker. Sis says mom was a party girl while my dad worked late hours, even when she was pregnant with me. Dad says mom cheated on him and he kicked her ass out of the house. Mom says she fled for her life after dad pulled a knife on her one night when she was late making dinner.

Hell, probably all of it is true. Like I care. Unfortunately, everyone wants me to pick sides: sis, mom, dad. They want me to agree with them when they call the others assholes. Mom likes to show me scars inflicted by dad. Dad's always hot to play me some recording where mom is apologizing and begging for him to take her back. And sis? She dropped out of school and none of us has heard from her since she turned eighteen and took off to San Francisco with her bassist boyfriend George.

Some days I can't help playing both sides against the middle. Neither of my folks can see that some battles are fought forever like the cowboys and Indians at each other's throats in the westerns on Sunday afternoon. They don't understand you can never truly win a fight, even when the other guy's dead.

******* ******* *******

Vegas strips down to nothing and dives in. He's already on his second lap of the quarry as I fold and refold my T-shirt, wishing I had a swimsuit or at least a pair of boxers that aren't light colored. Showoff. I know what has to be done if I don't want blondilocks to get the better of me. I look down at the dozing Wanda and damned if her eyes don't open a crack to check me out. I strip off my shorts and underwear and jump in. Feels great. I take a couple of unsteady strokes and find myself in the middle of the swimming hole with a view of both ends and the opposite bank. Three teenage girls at the far end of the quarry turn from Vegas' graceful strokes and point at me, two of them giggling and one looking as though she wants to hightail it out of there.

******* ******* *******

Slobber kept kicking my ass (when he could find me) all through junior high. When high school started though, I swore it'd be different. It was the first day of 10th Grade and I'd been fixing up my stepdad Bert's '77 El Dorado all summer so I wouldn't have to deal with Slobber and his army of sniveling psychopaths on the bus. Bert's a nice enough guy when he wasn't kicking my ass himself, good with cars and my mom.

Anyway, I drove in to school, a tad on the late side since I had to change a flat, and noticed most of the kids had already gone in for the first bell. All except Slobber sleeping on a bench on the edge of the parking lot, a shit-eating grin on his face. I looked down at my passenger seat and saw the chipped lug wrench still out from the change. I'm not sure if it was a revelation or what, but I imagined myself as a knight with the lug wrench as my lance. I placed a sweat sock over the end of the steel rod and tucked it in my jacket.

******* ******* *******

On the car ride home from the quarry, Vegas takes a short cut. By this time we're blitzed and no one seems to mind. I've got a wicked burn from lying out and a cut on my knee from diving off the top lip of the quarry to impress the girls who ended up leaving before I could ask them what they thought about my cannonball. Vegas must have scared them off, I guess.

Wanda tries to direct us back to Belson, but Vegas keeps switching dirt roads through the national forest until we're totally lost. I don't care much, one way or another. The old man isn't going to chew me out tonight, not if I can help it. The hell with his bullshit, anyway. I reach my hand into the back and start caressing the inside of Wanda's leg. I don't know why I think it's a good idea, I just do. I start at her knee and slowly work my way up to her thigh. Then her pussy. I play with it as dust and bits of clay shoot out in a long arc behind the churning tires.

Vegas hums tunelessly, having given up on the radio. His voice sounds faraway, echoing into the bottom of the last beer he's been clutching for dear life. For a second I think I recognize the tune—the Rocky theme song— but I'm not entirely sure until my hand touches his stiff fingers between Wanda's thighs. I look back and see her straddling the head rests of both our seats, her shorts hanging down over her left ankle. Vegas brakes to a stop and looks at me, then looks at the two of us stroking her legs and the lazy drunken grin on her face, then looks at me again.

"Come on...."

"What?"

"Come on." Vegas motions to the road and staggers outside. I follow. We circle around and sit on the hood, sharing the last warm beer.

"OK." He tips the bottom of the can up to the darkening sky and crushes it. "Paper, scissors, rock."

"Huh?"

"For who goes first."

"Oh...all right."

At this point, the flies start getting pretty bad, swarming around our heads, but I try to concentrate. I'd bet my last one hundred and thirty-five dollars that he isn't any smarter than me.

"We'll go on three...ready?"

Now he'd never allow himself to be cut in half. "One." So that leaves scissors or rock. "Two." So then, does he want to smash me or castrate me? "Three."

We flick our wrists. He has scissors. I have rock. He shrugs his shoulders and smiles. I swat at the flies and climb into the back seat through the passenger door. I struggle to get into position and Wanda shifts so that she's lying across the seat. I pull down my pants and push myself into her, closing my eyes. The few times I've had sex were all like this, drunken couplings with me feeling like an alien. She moans a little and I thrust harder, but worry about losing my erection. I feel nothing, like on the day I smashed Slobber twice on the face before going into school, breaking his eye socket and jaw. He was never the same after that. His eyes were closed and he never saw who did him dirty. Afterwards, I found myself wanting to tell him, "Don't blame yourself, you couldn't have known what I'd do." But the bully in him never came back.

The car engine rumbles to life. It lurches forward and accelerates down the dirt road. I pull myself off Wanda who looks as though she'd woken from a bad dream. I pull up my pants, she grabs her shorts.

"God-damn flies!" Vegas screams as he accelerates. The

car slides from side to side in the heavy dirt. "Fucking kid, doesn't even know how to have a gang bang."

The car skids around a tight turn and I find myself yelling, "Hey, it's my dad's car, I'll drive."

"Fuck you."

"I'll fucking drive."

"I should fucking kill you."

The Plymouth slams to a stop, but not before the front grill cracks into an elm just off the road. Vegas slumps over the driver's seat, banging his tired fists, streaked white from the quarry, on the steering column. He tumbles face first out of the car and I circle around to the driver's seat. I find myself saying, "I'm not such a bad guy, you know. I'll get you guys home."

I put my mind into piloting mode. Go straight, I tell myself, and you'll find a road you know. I slam the door shut and slap the car in reverse. It takes some doing, but the bumper finally untangles itself from the tree. I slap it into first, swoop off the shoulder and run over a log. Or something big. Hope the tires are OK. I keep my eyes peeled ahead of me, focusing on not falling asleep and getting home in one piece. By sheer force of will I steer us through the woods to County Road 543 and then take 72 West into town. I cross the 8th Street Bridge, pass the week-night crowd at The Howling Dog, and pull into my parking spot at the apartment complex.

"Told you I'd get us there," I say to the empty passenger seat. I stumble out the door and keep it open in case they want to follow. I shake Wanda awake and she looks around, confused. I think about asking her to my room, but before I can, she slips out of the back and stumbles toward the bar.

Where in the hell's blondilocks? Probably passed out in back, sleeping like a log. I check the floor and cushions, but he's nowhere to be seen. Impossible, unless he's fucking Houdini. I walk around the car and notice splotches of road kill on the tires and lug nuts, but no Vegas. He must have gotten out. Somehow. The car's empty now, anyway. Fuck him.

The bumper looks pretty bad, but I'll deal with it in the morning.

******* ******* *******

I wake to a hand nudging my back and poking my kidneys. I roll over, still dressed in last night's clothes, and look up square into the only loaded handgun in Belson. My apartment spins into focus.

My dad stands behind the officers, shaking his head. I figure the old man's just getting back at me for making his life hell. It's only fair, since I pulled this same stunt on him yesterday. "Don't blame yourself, you couldn't have known what I'd do," I tell him. My head throbs and the room swirls as I lean forward. The cops stare at me like I'm insane.

"Could you please point that somewhere else," dad says. "Accidents happen, you know. Maybe it wasn't his fault."

For some reason I find myself thinking about Vegas, the log I ran over, and the blood on the bumper.

"You have a lot of explaining to do, young man." The older officer grimaces. Chubby-wubby snorts derisively. My old man has a look of pain on his face. He's worried about me. He's actually worried. "I'll stand behind you, no matter what happens. Even jail," dad says. His face is bone white, as though he's seen a ghost.

I look around the room and almost feel sorry for the dread on my father's face and pity in the older cop's eyes. But the young cop's face surprises me—he's in shock, his mouth frozen in a grimace like the dead setter on the side of the road. Maybe these guys aren't so bad. Maybe they're not enemies after all.

"Christ, I didn't hurt him, did I?"

They don't answer, but they don't need to. Something tells me I'll be seeing Vegas everywhere I go.

Sugar, Wine, Smoke, and Glue

Sugar

I wasn't sure what to make of it when my daughter sat at the breakfast table with a cigarette butt in one hand and a Skittle in the other. Karen had attempted to hide them from me, clenching her tiny fists when I tried to pry open her fingers. Her stubbornness already surpassed both Francine's and mine: nap time was a war of wills, latched doors a minor inconvenience, and she threw a fit if there were even the remotest chance she might land candy out of the deal.

Sweets were poison in my book. The cough syrup I guzzled as a teenager to get through the monotony of high school ruined candy for me as an adult. I never knew what would trigger my violent reactions, but I made sure to avoid the following: juju bees, candied apples, Jordan almonds, yams, cotton candy, apple cider, and toothpaste.

The only thing that seemed to help me from throwing up when I smelled sweets were the cigarettes I started chain smoking soon after I married Francine. I don't blame her for my habit or for my inability to feel comfortable with a woman and, later, a child in my home. The fault was mine—I'd fallen into some sub-basement of fatherhood, where my Dad had spent his entire marriage drinking homemade wine in a combination rumpus room and workshop of his own creation. My own escape involved a deck off the kitchen that my wife and exuberant daughter quickly learned to avoid.

This wasn't to say I didn't love Karen. She meant the world to me—bright, energetic, and wise beyond her four years and two months should have made her. She had an openness that made me question everything about my own existence. In fact, she downright scared me at times.

Many of the memorable events in my life were foreshadowed by things my daughter either said or did. For example, just before my boss Mr. Yancy at the insurance company was fired for embezzlement, Karen said "Bossman Yancy take my candy," even though she'd never met him. And the morning before my fender bender with, of all people, a litigation attorney, Karen said, "Car go boom, Daddy." And so did my wallet. Francine and I stopped trying to spell out words around her. For example, my wife's recent suggestion: M-A-R-R-I-A-G-E C-O-U-N-S-E-L-O-R, led to Karen bawling for six straight hours.

My daughter looked on the verge of tears now as I massaged her knuckles and gently eased open her fingers. I snatched the Skittle and cigarette butt from her and walked away as the first sniffles started, tossing her "treasures" in the trash, but not before Fran noticed.

"Dan, you're ruining her childhood," she said before leaving the kitchen and joining Karen back at the table. Francine's own parents had been stern and unforgiving, something she made sure never to be with her daughter.

We were supposed to be Fran and Dan, the perfect Midwest couple with an open door and inviting smiles to welcome our child's future friends into our home. A couple with the singsong names that would roll off neighbors' tongues at barbecues. A couple that was not supposed to argue in whispers, first about finances and domestic roles, then about everything else.

Wine

I remember when my wife started sniping at me in earnest—the trouble rolled into our home the morning after last Thanksgiving. I'd argued with her parents all day and had ducked out from the festivities early to hang out on the deck. My lack of commitment to her "friction-free" holiday plans had made her angry beyond tossing the salad tongs into the stuffing. She glared at me and edged her chair closer to Karen, farther from me.

The next evening at dinner I noticed that Fran had decided to switch from beer to wine, not a dry cabernet, but a sickly sweet sherry she knew would nauseate me. She said nothing as she downed first one glass, then another. Even Karen noticed, saying, "Mommy mad." I took my dinner to the deck, the first of many to follow.

Perhaps this was her way of keeping me at arm's length. I wanted a big family that would invade every room and force me bubbling and effusive into the middle of it, but she was content with just a daughter—being an only child herself. Fran was also a career woman with no patience for losing ground to those around her who were less talented. An opinion I suspect that she was forming about me. She continually shifted from job to job, pitting her employers against one another for titles and salary. I was blatantly loyal and lacking in ambition. She called me her "starter husband" with mock affection.

There was no middle ground in our home divided between sugar and smoke. I couldn't stand to kiss her anymore, even after inhaling most of a pack before bedtime. While I attempted to stoically accept the tension, Francine threw herself into a revolving door of hobbies: yoga, macramé, kick-boxing, wine collecting and, most recently,

feng shui, which involved redecorating the house to max-
imize our "love" zones and tacking crystals above the mir-
rors in our bedroom.

She was creating a different "energy" in our home, and
part of this involved setting up separate twin beds in our
room to give ourselves "space." Distance in close proximi-
ty, a foreign concept to me, even under the auspices of an
ancient Chinese belief. But I agreed to the change, dope
that I was, and Karen gradually distanced herself from me
and her mother.

Smoke

One evening Fran visited me out on the deck after we
put our daughter to sleep. She had an intense look in her
eyes—one I'd seen often during the early years of our
marriage when she nuzzled next to me on the couch.

"What are we going to do?" she asked, pulling up a
lawn chair next to mine.

"About what?" I looked at the planks of the unfinished
pine deck, littered with leaves from the late October In-
dianapolis night.

"Karen deserves better," she slurred, taking my hand in
hers. The wine on her breath was heavy, but not as sweet as
usual. "Remember how we used to sit out here together?"

"Yes." I should have told her that I thought about it

practically every time I was out here—muggy summer nights, freezing winter afternoons, rain-soaked spring mornings. Back when we were still Francine and Daniel.

"Do you smell that?" she asked.

"It's old man Hanson. Burning leaves."

"This time of night?"

"He doesn't have anyone," I said. "He can do whatever he wants."

"I can feel the heat from his backyard even from here."

"We're becoming our parents," I said, twisting the brittle body of a leaf, the dry husk separating in my fingers.

"Let's go to bed," she said and dragged me up from my seat, the end of my cigarette still curling smoke into the cool autumn night.

Glue

It's surprising how some memories stay with you like a mole you hate or a scar you grow to love. When I woke that morning next to Francine in my bed, I knew that something was wrong. I immediately thought of the legendary starling that had flown into my parents' house when I was a child and got stuck in my sister's hair. I opened my eyes and stared directly into Francine's thoughtful look.

"You want another child, don't you?" I said, smiling. "Why else would you come to bed with me?"

"You're an asshole."

She tried to roll over and yelped. I felt a sharp tug on the roots of my hair. We were somehow attached.

"Jesus Christ," I said, running my hand up to where our hair was joined and feeling her own fingers patting an impossibly large wad of bubble gum.

"You're a pig," she said. "This doesn't surprise me."

"You can blame the liquor at least. I went to bed with you sober."

"Mommy? Daddy?"

We tilted our heads and saw Karen leaning against the foot of the bed with gum wrappers strewn at her feet. We tried standing, but it was too painful. We couldn't manage to work together well enough to reach our feet. Finally, we collapsed back on the pillow, attached from forehead to neck, her shoulder-length strands enmeshed in mine.

"Karen, honey, can you get Daddy's beard scissors from the bathroom and bring them out here?"

"Dan, she's only four."

"Do you want to get out of this or not?"

We tried not to look at each other as we waited for Karen to return.

"I'm growing bald. It won't grow back," I said.

"I just got a hundred dollar haircut."

"I've got a meeting on Monday."

"I'm a woman. Besides, yours stinks like smoke."

Karen crawled in bed with the tiny scissors and wiggled up to the headboard between us.

"Go ahead, Karen," I said. "Cut away."

"Karen, honey, why don't you decide whose hair you'd rather cut. Mommy's," she said sternly, shaking her head, "or Daddy's," she said sweetly.

The longer Karen paused the more it forced me to notice the nearly forgotten fragrance of my wife underneath the smoke, wine, and lingering musk of last night's lovemaking. She smelled like home.

Fran smiled. "Cut Daddy's hair, honey. Won't he look funny with weird hair?"

Karen reached up and snipped away at the smoke and wine in equal measure until she was the only thing left between us.

The Diary of Spidey-Bat

Monday

OK, so just how did a formerly productive member of society with a graduate degree in writing end up putting on a half-assed superhero costume for tips? One word: Hollywood. It's an all-powerful evil entity that chews people up from all walks of lives, all ages. On the bus bench outside my apartment, Leon from Hoboken recites Shakespeare in a British accent, and claims mastery of archery, horse riding, and yodeling. If you haven't already guessed it, Leon had once been a working actor with a pretty good agent, then an agent that specialized in magic acts, and now he himself was an agent of terror for the nannies, students, and working class families looking for a place to sit while taking the LA public transit system.

Leon scares the crap out of me. Not physically. He's my doppelganger. Crap, I suppose my harbinger. See, I am already starting to lose my handle on the meaning of words, my useless degree proudly framed over my beer bottle cap collection. Instead of writing poetry, the not-so-sucky American novel, or even sarcastic ad copy sprinkled with a pinch of malaise, I've pickled my senses mastering the art of the screenplay. Like Leon, I started by perfecting my craft: books, courses, conferences. I developed quickly paced scenes with snappy patter and utilized character archetypes to move my plot forward. I placed my screenplays in a few contests and landed an agent old enough to be my father, then buried my father from cancer, then discovered two years later that my so-called agent had placed my scripts in envelopes that never got sent around town. It was a case of senility or early retirement. By the time it all got sorted out, I had somehow become old news at that particular agency. What the hell?

Several years later, I landed myself a manager/producer in a Century City high rise, who convinced me to rework my screenplay about Houdini's son into a Vegas bachelor buddy comedy that he hated and I hated. He didn't even let me go from the agency…he just stopped taking my calls like every woman I'd ever asked to move in with me.

It was then that I started to take matters into my own hands. Why not shop my own work? I networked for screenwriting gigs through my writer's day job (managing a strip club). There was constant drama as I tried to fulfill my dreams by sucking up to washed-up Hollywood has-beens, transforming their tawdry ideas into viable scripts in the morning hours after kicking the latest stripper out with high-heel shoes and a power bar. My father worried about me, but not enough to fly across country and drag me back home to Normal, Illinois, where my bedroom was as I had left it in my post-college flight to find my fortune.

All in all, I optioned five screenplays and was paid less than twenty grand for ten years of work. I'm not even sure where the time went. I ended up tracking time by genres: the year of the robotic sci-fi thriller, the police action dramedy, the mutant teen horror. For some reason, my girlfriends always seemed to match the project of the moment, a string of strippers scared to live a real life (just like myself). Then, the economy tanked.

With ten years of nothing but working in shady establishments, I could not seem to get a job at a respectable bar or restaurant to save my life. Odd jobs carried their own form of peril. There were the two accidents I got into as a limo driver. The worst was the time I played the role of Darth Vader (with a fake lightsaber) as part of the entertainment at a kid's birthday party, and got cracked in the ribs by a snot-nosed kid (with a real baseball bat).

Nate, the dude who played Luke Skywalker and the proprietor of *Birthday on Wheels,* disappeared on me, probably afraid I'd sue him.

Recovering from this injury, I met a Filipina waif of a girl at our local Hollywood coffee shop Beano. Maria was a massage therapist and Tarot reader who took a liking to me, moving into my studio apartment the next day to save money, and called me her "artist." Everything was awesome in a year-long relationship that was the best of my life. We enjoyed cheap wine, reality TV, and easy conversation. At least until my unemployment extension finally ran out.

Then the trifecta hit: my Miata bumper fell off, my new girlfriend left me a good-bye note on my unwashed counter, and my #2 incisor had to be yanked by a dental student at USC. Needless to say, I lived month-to-month, and I now needed a plan to make some dough or I'd be on the street looking to share a bench duplex with Leon. The call to Dad, a widower who spent his time at the VFW recounting semi-heroic times in the Army with his buddies, loomed as a one-way ticket back home to Normal, Illinois. I didn't want to admit that I was a colossal failure and I sure didn't want to go back to bunk in my childhood bedroom with super hero posters still on the walls.

That's when the idea of Spidey-Bat came to me. With a costume, I could join the throng of other superheroes on Hollywood Boulevard looking for tips from picture-taking tourists. I had seven days to make my rent. It wasn't a good plan, but it was a plan. Problem was that I was too depressed to move. I lay in bed watching a *Doctor Who* marathon, thinking that it might help me figure out who I was and needed to be. Time seemed endless watching a series about a time lord, and the day and night somehow passed away.

Tuesday

OK, so I finally got out of my apartment to trek the five blocks over to Hollywood Boulevard in my Spidey-Bat costume. Of course, it took longer than usual in order to make sure I didn't get run over crossing the street with limited visibility through eye slits. The only requirement in choosing my costume was to make sure that it had a full mask so that no one, especially Maria, would recognize how low I'd sunk. So how did I settle on something as dumb as a Spidey-Bat? For starters, it fit my budget as I found the requisite pieces of the costume in my studio apartment.

Several months ago, a couch-surfing former college roommate stayed at my place. He was a bit of a freak (some things never change) and he was unable to hide his full-on Batman fetish. He slept fully decked-out for crime fighting and Maria caught him on the floor early one morning masturbating with his little batman. This incident cut his LA visit short and he accidentally left his Batman boots, pants, and utility belt beneath the futon.

The superhero costume top was from the most recent Halloween when I had convinced Maria to play Maria Jane to my Spideyman. However, it was another Mary Jane, from too many bong tokes, that was to blame for me losing my spider pants that night at a rocking house party in my apartment complex.

When I passed my coffee joint Beano, Maria was there talking to the head barista Chuck she'd started to see after me, as though having an income was important. I hurried past them onto the strip, and it didn't take me long to find a free spot to set up shop among the other costumed figures on Hollywood Boulevard between Mann's Chinese Theater and the Kodak Theater.

I sized up my competition and tried to make sense about how they went about asking for tips. There was Zorro, who worked in tandem with a Dirty Bert from Sesame Street, drawing in the biggest crowds. The tourist girls hugged Zorro, while the children and Asian businessmen posed with Bert. A miniature Godzilla planted himself on his own star, next to a scary-looking Marilyn Monroe, Darth Vader, Shrek, and the blue-skinned girl from Avatar. To the east, the characters from Marvel ruled to the corner of Highland with three Spidermen, Thor, Ironman, and a skinny Hulk with a Mexican wrestling mask. To the west, the DC characters gathered with two Batmen (one big, one little), Green Lantern, Superman, and Wonder Woman who roped in the male tourists with an actual lasso.

I posed on an empty star in an alcove outside the subway entrance that gave me more room to operate. Yes, this would be as good a home as any for Spidey-Bat. It must have been obvious that I felt out of place because Dirty Bert strolled over to me and said, "Shove off, piss ant—you can't be both Marvel and DC."

I thought about that for a moment. Dirty Bert had a point. I was unique, which might be good for marketing. But to sell it I would need to create a genesis for my hero, a story that would make murdered parents and radioactive spider bites seem tame in comparison. Besides, Dirty Bert freaked me out a bit.

I decided that I needed to head home to gather my backstory, my motivation, and the last half bottle of Jose Cuervo stashed under the kitchen sink for just such an emergency. On my way out, I thought I caught a couple of smirks. Dirty Bert waved at me with his middle finger and his companion Zorro sliced a Z with a plastic rose before mouthing "loser" and planting his free hand on the lower back of a hot Swedish backpacker.

What did I do? I gathered up my wounded pride, and headed home.

Wednesday

OK, so now that my carefully crafted backstory was iron-clad I figured that it would be easy to gather a crowd. What tourist or child of a tourist wouldn't want to hear the story about how Spiderman and Batman left their homes to join together on a mission to save every known universe from a time traveling villain. Yes, they did succeed. We're all alive, aren't we? No, they did not get to return home as their forms were caught in a black hole, molded into a single entity, and sent to the one place that needed a hero more than anywhere else in the cosmos. Yes, our earth!

At my appointed spot, on one of the few empty stars, I passionately shared my genesis and soon ran into a language barrier. Even the tourists who understood English didn't quite get the science behind my epic genesis. It was impossible to pitch it in the second or two it took to get their attention before they passed by.

It was then that Jack Sparrow, of all people, came to my rescue. Even though his character (in the movies) was a bit selfish, he gave me a high five and began the most amazing Spidey-Bat rap: "Two heroes in one suit, with red mask and black boots, this cat is where it's at, the amazing Spidey-Bat!" I know the actual words might sound lame, but Jack had a booming voice and a great way of drawing attention to my alcove. So what did I do? Well, I danced…kind of. I attacked the air with some pretty choice moves, and some bear of a dude wearing a much-too-small Harley Davidson T-shirt put his arm around me while his three kids posed for photos, dancing with me and punching the air to the rap.

I started singing the words to my own song, as I stashed the crumpled bill in my utility belt. I only had $995 to go to make rent before Monday! But now, it totally seemed possible. Jack Sparrow ended up being a pretty good dude and insisted we didn't reveal our names just like real heroes. It was his first week, too. He was an aspiring actor (shocking I know) and was doing this as a way to get extra spending money to go on a rafting trip to Thailand. He drew in crowds for me with his rapping and banter, and I lined up girls for him by pretending I was scared of him and his "big sword" (OK a bit phallic perhaps).

It became obvious that we were now a force to be reckoned with. Batman and little Batman came by to show off their choreographed fake fight sequence and to call us amateurs and posers. Storm Trooper hid behind a trashcan and pointed his weapon at us, making a *pshew pshew* sound that could have been a laser gun I suppose. Marilyn hit on Jack, and that caused him to take off to use the bathroom a few times in order to ditch her advances as she might have been born in the same year as the actual Marilyn Monroe.

During one of Jack's absences, Zorro came by with the rose that he brandished like a sword to draw in the women and slapped me upside my mask to get my attention. Dirty Bert nodded from the gym entrance where he was talking to a bodybuilder, and I was having a hard time figuring out what was going on until Zorro said: "That will be twenty percent."

"Excuse me," I said.

"Jesus, you're dense. Here's the lowdown—all the regulars give me and Bert a cut of everything they make. It keeps things peaceful and provides you with protection. For example, Disney characters just tend to disappear. Your friend is the fifth Jack Sparrow this month to show up… and none of them have returned."

"You must think I'm some sort of asshole," I said, and got mad when Zorro grinned in response. My pal Jack appeared on the scene sipping a bottled water from the Fresh and Easy Mart and Zorro sneered, "There's only room for one dashing swashbuckler here!" before joining Dirty Bert at the gym entrance. What a nut job this guy was thinking he could muscle us out of a percentage of our tips.

Still, for some reason, I didn't tell Jack about the incident. He was on fire drawing in the crowds…and I didn't want to mess with the mojo. We made bank that day—

after twelve hours I'd managed to rake in four hundred bucks. Even better, Jack explained how the good ones pair up on the strip, and to treat the experience like prison, to avoid the warring cliques.

That, of course, was my cue to ask him what he went to prison for. I think I figured it out later that night when he took me out to a downtown loft party in my Spidey-Bat costume to see some of his customers. He was an E dealer, and convinced me to join him and a group of strangers to drop a tab together. Now this sounded a bit dangerous, but I was a super hero after all.

It was weird to be rolling with a bunch of strangers nearly half my age, but the narcotic had its desired affect and anonymous strangers became anonymous friends. I didn't seem out of place in my costume as many of the people there had gone to art school or were musicians…I even got one girl (at least I hope it was a girl) to take me into a broom closet.

The night got hazy after that as I drank too much. I remembered laughing at some point when I passed out condoms and lube from the bat utility belt that my pal must have left in there. I think we blew up the condoms like balloons and everyone got a bit sticky with the bat lube. Did we end up somewhere eating waffles? Not sure. Finally, I felt the light stabbing into my eyes as a pirate dropped me back at my apartment and into my bed.

Thursday

Epic hangover.

Friday

Hangover. How can it last two days? It sucks getting older. Something always hurts a little more than it used to, and that includes old wounds. My older sister Lorraine thought I was a too much of a dreamer for my own good, and once hid my boyhood diary in her bra drawer to make me want to go out and play with other kids. That didn't stop me, and led to one of our worst fights. She never understood that I liked the anonymity of observation, which made the masked hero such a freeing idea. In the suit, I had met tons of people, and partied with kids that normally would have thought me a bit lame. I felt like there was some lesson here that I needed to learn, and I was eager to get my ass back to work.

Ahhh…the best laid plans. I returned to my blank star and noticed that my pal Jack Sparrow was nowhere to be seen. Perhaps, he was taking the day off or else he was on his way to Thailand. It wasn't long before Zorro came by with his stupid plastic rose and made the sign of a knife slitting a throat with it. "I warned you," was all that he or anyone else said to me that day.

Maybe I was being paranoid, but it seemed as though all of the other characters kept a wide berth around me. Was I being blacklisted? More than once, I saw Dirty Bert whispering in the ear holes of masked crusaders or painted vixens, pointing to me. It was a good thing that I had that rap song to fall back on. I danced like I was still on E, and attacked the air until I felt like I was going to pass out in that polyester spider top. The maneuvers worked…kind of. I ended up making about half that day what I had with Jack, and couldn't help but wonder if he was in a mass grave somewhere with hundreds of other Jacks Sparrows, Goofies, and Little Mermaids, the victim of some secret Disney-funded hit squad.

By the time the sun started pinking, I was wiped from not eating enough and being overheated. I was just about to take off when I saw a nightmare walking toward me. It was Maria with her loser barista boyfriend Chuck strolling down the street hand-in-hand. What kind of name was Chuck…he was blond, bearded, and overweight…she should have called him upchuck. She couldn't be happier with this ass, could she? I was jealous and wanted this jerk to feel the same pain I did. A plan came to me and I acted with a hero's reflexes. I hurried over to Zorro and threw down the gauntlet of a challenge: I bet him $20 that he wasn't suave enough to get a kiss from that hot Asian chick holding hands with a bearded loser.

Zorro laughed and flipped his shoulder-length locks. He strode up to the couple, holding out his plastic rose and offering a kiss to "the most dazzling lady in all the land." Maria smiled at the compliment, and Chuck looked like he had swallowed a fly. Then the impossible happened. My former girlfriend sighed and shook her head, handing back the rose. Did she actually like that turd? Zorro sneered at me and said, "I never took that bet, loser."

Yes I was a loser, and I was sick of it!

Chuck grinned like a young virile Santa and took Maria's hand in his. He led her down the boulevard ultra-slow, rubbing it in with a victory lap. He would no doubt take her for a hot night of street tacos and sex at his pad to reality TV shows. So what if that big shot could pay for cable? What about me? My whole life was slipping away...but only if I let it.

I was a hero now, and I took action. I snatched the rose out of Zorro's hand with my left and cold-cocked Chuck with my right. It hurt like hell, but was worth it. The barista lost his balance and collapsed face-first onto the sidewalk, pulling Maria down with him. Just like the hit men who killed Batman's parents, I tossed the rose onto Chuck's ass, and stepped back into my shadowy alcove.

Zorro walked up to try to lend a dashing hand and Chuck sprung up, crushing him in a bear hug. "Maria, call the cops," he said, squeezing the swashbuckler in his arms with serious intent…like a blackhead pimple.

What did I do? I got the hell out of there. The very last thing I heard was Chuck yelling: "What do you mean it was Spidey-Bat? You asshole, there is no such thing!"

Saturday

I had become a legend on the boulevard. Apparently, Zorro had been cuffed and taken to the Hollywood Police station. Dirty Bert hadn't shown up yet for the first time in months according to Spiderman #2, and I felt a bit like Dorothy after the Wicked Witch had been melted.

Sponge Bob pulled out a breakfast croissant from his square pants (no I didn't eat it) and it was only the beginning of the tribute. Old Marilyn offered me a "Frenchie"— what the hell?—that I politely refused. Little Batman and Batman saluted me with a two-man Pyramid that brought us all a bit of attention, and tips. I was suddenly big man on campus for the first time, well, ever! The whole area around the subway funneled crowds to my alcove, and I was no longer getting Zorro's leftovers. At this rate, rent wouldn't be a problem. I was even thinking about grabbing lunch with Wonder Woman, who had been trying to rope me all morning.

She wasn't bad looking even if she was taller than me

in boots and had surprisingly muscular shoulders. Perhaps my mojo had returned? Then the incident happened. Dirty Bert emerged from the subway like a vampire from the crypt, stomping with oversized furry feet straight toward me. Time stopped, just like in an action movie, and every creature in homespun outfits, sequins, and leather froze to watch the showdown.

The success I'd had with Chuck wasn't all luck. I had worked for three months in a Tae Bo studio, and readied myself to launch a front kick that could theoretically drive my nemesis back to Sesame Street. This weirdo couldn't be packing, could he? How could he hold a weapon with those furry mitts?

No, I was the amazing Spidey-Bat. Nothing could hurt me…nothing except for the secret weapon Dirty Bert had prepared all morning.

You see, Zorro had been the muscle of the operation, and Dirty Bert was nothing but a fetishist and a drunk. After visiting Zorro in the holding tank, he went on a bender. Dirty Bert did something unthinkable. He took off his head mask by yanking on his zippered unibrow, revealing a mustached creep with pale skin and acne scars. If I thought the unwashed stench rising from the neck hole was rank, it did little to prepare me for what came next.

Dirty Bert had a gift. He projectile-vomited the night's drinks, the morning's drinks, and his McDonald's breakfast onto me. It smelt like he pissed, yacked, and oozed his small intestines right into my facemask, which did not stop the liquid from burning my eyes, filling my nostrils, and causing me to dry heave. My eye slits filled with mucus and I would have screamed except for fear of swallowing it.

I couldn't stand it. The boozy egg stench was too much. I had to unmask, but what about my secret identity? My pride? Before Mom died of cancer she used to call me her little hero. I thought of that moment often, when I had my back to the wall, and dug deep to find a way, any way, to keep my dream alive.

I spied a Popeye's chicken bag that several pigeons had been pecking—those cannibals! I picked it up, took off my mask, and stuffed the bag over my head. Through the tattered holes, I could make out Dirty Bert laughing and a large German tourist yelling in horror at the fight Spidey-Bat had lost. I suddenly had cramps and would surely toss my cookies if I could not get out of this costume. For the second time in two days, I fled, running as fast as I could without my makeshift mask flying off into the confused crowd of onlookers.

Sunday

It's surprising how quickly you can go from hero to goat.

When I returned to my star early the next morning, Zorro was back and the first to come up with my alternate rap song: "Spidey-Chicken, Spidey-Chicken, he'll run from any ass-kicking." Storm Trooper must have been an actor because he made the most lifelike chicken noises to accommodate the song, and all of the gang flapped their wings whenever I was near. Tiny Godzilla did the chicken dance and that caused Old Marilyn to fall off one of her high heels and she had to steady herself on Sponge Bob's suspenders.

Apparently, Dirty Bert and Zorro had regained their status as top dogs. I wouldn't have come back except that I needed a few more greenbacks to make rent. One good thing had come out of this already. Last night, I called my sister to ask her advice on how to get puke out of my superhero costume, and she didn't even judge me. We weren't on the phone long, but she advised me to treat my costume like a carpet (since I couldn't afford to dry clean). I bought a special cleaner to soak up the vomit, then vacuumed it off. It was gross, and looked like wet saw dust in my Dirt Devil, but I finally got the costume in good enough shape to be able to come back (even if the egg smell still lingered).

I also had a new plan. I had brought along some adhesive and black Magic Marker in my bat belt, and stenciled Spidey-Bat on my own star, figuring that it would catch the attention of the crowd. I was right. Quite a few tourists snapped pics of me and my walk-of-fame star. I was able to make rent money after only a few hours. The other heroes didn't like my new tactic, not one bit.

Zorro led the scariest of the curb creatures to confront me about it, too, including skinny Hulk grunting with a wrestling mask: "No star for you!" My Spidey-Bat senses must have been working overtime because I felt an incredible sense of danger. And I was right. Just then, the Hollywood Police made a raid, with three wagons pulling up curbside and a squad of police started rounding up heroes. A few lucky ones on the ends of the block took off, and I understood why the subway was a big advantage when Dirty Bert and Zorro raced down the escalator.

I stopped to pull up the adhesive, and it took just long enough for me to get nabbed by a female officer pointing a taser at my nutsack, looking eager to have a story to tell her pals about. I held up my hands, and she cuffed them behind my back with with a plastic tie. It was pandemonium as parents tried to shield the eyes of children crying because their heroes were being arrested. I was escorted onto the street, where the sergeant in charge looked me over.

"Christ, he's not Marvel and he's not DC," the police veteran muttered, pointing to the first two wagons where the Batmen and Spidermen were being separated and led to different vehicles.

"And he's not an independent," the policewoman behind me said, and I looked into the third van which was being filled with Old Marilyn, Sponge Bob, Godzilla, and Shrek. "Where should I put him?"

"We've got strict orders on segregation. I don't want to hear it from the Captain if there's a brawl because we couldn't keep these creeps under control."

I was having a hard time following this, but I thought I saw an opening. "Hello, officer, I just wanted to let you know that the Amazing Spidey-Bat is retiring from crime fighting!"

Storm Trooper made a clucking noise on his way to the third van, and I hoped this interruption hadn't ruined my plea.

"You smell," the sergeant said. "I don't want you riding in my squad car. It's your lucky day, dimwit. You can go."

I didn't wait for him to change his mind. I hurried across the street, away from the raid, and didn't even care that my hands were still fastened behind my back. I was free. I could pay rent. I had another month to make my mark.

First thing was first. I headed to Beano, hoping that Maria was there to cut me loose. Or perhaps Chuck or one of the other baristas could use a bagel knife to set me free. I felt like I was hero enough to take on the world as I shouldered my way through the gawkers and tourists. Dad would be happy to not get the call he'd been dreading for years, and perhaps I had enough leftover money to invite Maria to a flick. Perhaps, my luck was changing. Over my shoulder, I could see the crooked white teeth of the Hollywood Sign beaming down on me.

Layover

A blue cloud—that's what her mother called it. A dreamlike bliss where problems flutter past like butterflies and everything is bathed in golden light.

Lyda Agnos rescrewed the cap on her almost empty bottle of Valium and tossed it into the graveyard of her purse. She pressed the button on her chair arm and reclined as far as the stiff airliner seat could move in the cramped first row. Lyda always booked herself into the front section of coach, where mothers with young children usually sat. She figured it was safer to be with children. *They* would never plummet to their screaming deaths in a fireball of metal and petrol.

Lyda was so paranoid about flying she was beginning to get paranoid that others could see her paranoia. She was a mess and she knew it, even with the Valium. It would be easier on everyone involved if she hated Peter. That's the thing about hatred. It can give you the strength to crawl out of bed when more fickle emotions let you down. If he had cheated on her or beat her, it might have saved them both a lot of grief.

Their daughters, parents, and friends wanted to blame someone for what happened. They didn't understand she and Peter were both to be pitied. He'd never had it in him to give of himself. And she long ago sucked dry what few emotions he had to offer over a decade of her life down the drain. It was hard not to be bitter.

Thirteen years. She tried to tell herself it would end up being her lucky number. Deep down, she doubted it. She didn't, couldn't, trust her instincts anymore. The subtle and not-so-subtle precepts she based her life on had peeled away, revealing shadows with no more substance than whispered promises between lovers. She kneaded her fingers into the chair arm and breathed in deeply. She rubbed the plastic arm, waiting for the blue cloud from the Valium to envelope her like an all-powerful genie from a magic lamp.

Planes never used to frighten her. The trouble started her junior year of college, the night before she was supposed to fly home to Berkeley for Christmas break. She stayed up late at a post-finals party with Peter, a year before he asked her to marry him. Peter's friends weren't radicals, but their parties tended to draw people who ate too much sugar as children. On this fateful night, a bearded man who called himself Blue Bart staked himself at the door and played the jovial host, jabbering nonsense and taking coats.

When Lyda arrived on the scene, Blue Bart muttered, "Congratulations," and handed her ten hits of acid. She wasn't big on psychedelics and didn't want a hangover for her morning flight home. But she also had a poor college student's mentality coupled with a Protestant's irrational desire to sew worn clothes and clean her plate. Lyda tucked the strip of colored paper in her sock for safekeeping and joined the festivities. Someone she knew would surely want them.

Later that evening, when she returned to her apartment with Peter, her skin tingled and she was short of breath. "I don't feel at all tired," she told him, sitting dutifully on the edge of the bed and undressing. She peeled off her socks and stared in confusion at the purple blotches on the inside of her ankle. She looked up to find Peter looming over her. "Oh God, that was stupid," he admonished, just as she remembered that warm, moist places tend to be conducive breeding grounds for psychedelic mischief.

An hour before her flight, she was still tripping, perhaps even beginning to peak, although it was difficult to tell on that much acid. That flight home redefined fear in Lyda's mind. She couldn't approach an airport now without remembering the plane constricting around her, convulsing like a rubber band in the hands of an epileptic madman.

Golden light, golden light, please, please, please, Lyda mouthed, mentally surrounding the plane in a safe, warm glow. She shifted her gaze from the plastic window shade blocking the overcast night sky. The well-tanned man in the aisle seat unbuttoned his suit coat and loosened his red tie. He was drinking a double gin and tonic and reading an airline magazine article on out-of-the-way Maui vacation spots. The precision and certainty of his movements comforted Lyda. He stripped the dark blue blazer from his shoulders and placed it on the arm of the empty middle seat between them.

"Hope you don't mind," he said with a slight Southeastern accent. He was probably from Atlanta, where she was scheduled to switch planes.

"It's a free country," she said, surprised to hear the flirtatiousness in her voice.

"That's a matter of opinion," he bantered.

"Or perspective."

She turned her shoulder and nestled her head into the small airliner pillow, the Valium fatigue suddenly overtaking her. As she drifted above the river of sleep on her wispy blue cloud, she thought about the discomfort of her friends. Although they were liberal-minded, her recent breakup was an unappreciated topic of conversation. They all knew the score. Married couples hang out with married couples.

She wondered if her flight to Baltimore to see Julia, her best friend from childhood, was a step forward or back. They had gradually grown apart since Lyda married, but still traded letters back and forth across the heartland. She hoped her oldest friend could help her mend a heart wounded long ago when her shaking hand had plunged a knife into her wedding cake.

Her blue Valium cloud drifted higher above the gushing waters of her fears and hopes. The river below trickled into a serene ocean of sleep, calm on the surface, but with the shadows of sharks hovering below the ripples of her thoughts, waiting for her to come crashing down.

****** ****** ******

Crashing. The word was on her lips as she jerked awake. She stifled a cry and looked around the plane. Everything was...oh Christ. The pillow behind her head just moved.

She slid away from the lap of the man in the aisle seat, causing his eyes to flutter open. Her purse was on the floor and the chair arms that divided the center seat had been raised so she could stretch out. He blinked as if he too was having a difficult time placing where he was.

"Nice sleep?" he asked with a yawn.

"Uh huh," Lyda responded, not knowing what to say. Had he taken liberties with her while she slept or had she scooted over next to him? "Ummm?" she began, but couldn't quite bring herself to be blunt.

"You were out almost three hours. We're in a holding pattern over Atlanta airport, about twenty minutes or so until we land." He shrugged his shoulders and turned his head to stare out the opposite window.

She considered raising her own blind, then thought better of it. Her teeth clenched and her palms were clammy. She felt awkward, like a schoolgirl trying to figure out the cat and mouse rules of dating. Trouble was, even when she had dated, she either wanted to sleep with someone or kill them in the first hour.

He turned back to her, leaned over, and said, "No matter how many times I see a sunrise at 10,000 feet, I never get used to it." Lyda caught a glimpse of orange streaks lighting up the clouds over his shoulder. "So Lyda," he continued in a more conversational tone. "How long did you say you were laying over in Atlanta?"

"Five hours," she said hesitantly. Well, that nailed it. He knew her name.

"Shitty connection."

She tried to remember what she had done in her fog to pique his interest. Although he was cute in a businessman sort of way, she was wary of involvement. Besides, she hadn't slept with anyone but her husband in thirteen years. That is, except for an unimportant one-night fling after the birth of Annie, her youngest.

The stranger smiled a little boy smile she found difficult to resist. "You know, I have a place not twenty minutes from the airport. You should come over and have a home-cooked Southern breakfast before moving on."

"Sure," she said. It looked as though she had made up her mind about him, whatever his name was.

The seat belt light flashed and they began their descent. Lyda's heart caught in her throat and she swallowed her last two Valium dry. Takeoffs and landings were the worst. Her hands shook and the stewardesses leered at her with blurry faces. A flashback of that acid trip was always a possibility. She took the stranger's tanned hand in hers.

"So what do your friends call you?" she asked.

"Nick," he answered, a little confused.

When she was in her early twenties, this question saved her from more than one embarrassing memory lapse the next morning.

"So, what do your friends call you?" he asked.

I'm not sure my friends would know me now, she thought as the concrete and greenery of the city rose up to meet their plane.

******** ******* ********

Less than an hour later she was nestling in a Jacuzzi like it was God's own womb, comforted by jets of water massaging her crimped neck. She was naked and not at all embarrassed by it. Her hippy mother still walked around the house au naturel and Lyda long ago lost any discomfort with disrobing in front of strangers. If she hadn't wanted Nick to get ideas of sexual intimacy, she might have donned the set of black underwear she packed in her overnight bag. But she didn't really care what he thought. Or if they fooled around. She was more enraptured by the hot bubbles pricking her skin.

An oversized picture window opened up to a small forest of scrawny evergreens bordering a carefully mowed back yard. From the enclosed deck, she scanned the living room of his two-story house and noted a woman's touch: vinyl-covered furniture, half-dead flowers filling the vases, all-matching furniture in a palette of teal, bronze, and purple. Her live-in-girlfriend alarm was set off by the color-coordinated art and furniture. Very few straight men would notice or care about such a minute detail.

Least of all Peter who walked through life in a haze or perhaps he actually saw it that way: shadow car, shadow house, shadow wife. Each curve and blackened edge interchangeable. He hadn't covered his tracks well. Lyda could tell when he lost himself in his private world where every woman was lover, daughter, mother. When the strange women began leaving messages for a guy named Keith, she knew what it meant, although she had to wait for the phone company to send past statements of the bill Peter paid every month. She wasn't shocked. She could live with the fact that he was a phone sex junkie. It did, however, bother her that he didn't have the balls to use his real name. Keith? Was that the person he thought he was underneath?

She felt something bump against her lips and caught a faint whiff of cilantro. She was momentarily startled by an oblong object under her chin, then realized it was Nick holding a miniature andouille sausage. So this is what he had been up to in the kitchen. She choked back a laugh even as she devoured his offering. She wondered if he thought nibbling on this little phallus was some sort of turn on. Nick set down a platter of sausage and cut-up cantaloupe on the lip of the whirlpool. He wore white boxers with hearts. She didn't even try to choke it back. She guffawed loudly.

"What?" he asked in embarrassment as he slid off his boxers and joined her in the water. "Did I miss something?"

"No, I'm just happy I'm not reading a bad mystery novel and eating a ten dollar airport croissant."

"Well, I hope you enjoy the eats and..." he added for good measure, "the Southern hospitality."

He lowered himself slowly into the Jacuzzi, pausing, as all men do, at the point where his genitals first touched the water. He winced slightly, then shimmied onto the ridge across from her. Lyda could tell he hadn't expected to get this far with her. His earlier debonair facade had been stripped away with his clothing. He prodded the underside of her knee with his big toe and broke into a lumbering flirtation, "So, you're a Leo, right?"

Lyda said nothing, just nodded.

"Well, I'm an Aries."

Lyda found herself wishing he would shut up before he said something too stupid for her to feel good about staying. She was just beginning to forget about her problems and didn't want her only tranquility in weeks to be ruined by his lame attempts to woo her.

"And I think that's supposed to make us a perfect match, right? We're both sun signs, you can tell 'cause when we mix with water, we get all this steam."

His arms lifted flamboyantly and his fingers splayed outward in the rising vapor like a Buddha in heat.

Lame, lame, lame, Lyda thought.

He bit his lip nervously and slid over to her side. Lyda held up her hand like a traffic cop flagging down a speeding motorist. Something wasn't adding up. It was obvious Nick didn't know the first thing about astrology.

"So how do you know I'm a Leo?" she asked, for the moment stopping his telegraphed advance.

"You were born on August 6th, that makes you a Leo right? Or are you a Libra?"

She knew she hadn't told Nick when her birthday was.

"You looked through my purse, didn't you?" she asked, appraising his face carefully.

Nick swallowed, then nodded.

Lyda glared at him. He should have known better. Never mess with a girl from Berkeley when it comes to astrology.

"Well, you were out like a light. You didn't wake up when the waitress, uh, stewardess, came so I was just checking to see if you were on any medication to...see if you were sick...or something."

You asshole, she thought.

"You asshole," came an answering echo from the front of the house.

Nick's expression became even more guilt stricken, if that were possible.

"Open up, you asshole," repeated the enraged woman.

"Oh shit, it's Yolanda!"

"Who's Yolanda?" Lyda asked as she sprang out of the water and covered her breasts with her arms. Her nonchalance about nakedness didn't include miffed girlfriends.

"My wife. We're separated, kind of."

Or wives. In a way, the situation made a sick kind of sense. Maybe her friends back home were right to fear her. She was obviously a marital bad luck charm.

"I brought the cops and a court order," Yolanda hollered. "Either you let me in or we're breaking down the door."

"Nick, what's going on here?"

"Don't worry about a thing," he said, rolling out of the Jacuzzi and toweling himself off. He threw on a pair of jeans and ran to a closet in the foyer. "Hide in here until I get rid of her."

"I don't get it. We weren't doing anything," Lyda protested as she shuffled to where he was pointing and stepped into a closet filled with coats. Nick shut the door and everything went black. The muscles in her back and neck that had begun to loosen up immediately tensed again.

She found herself stressing out about her daughters, whom she already missed, and, unfortunately—Peter. Just after their breakup, her ex had a minor heart attack, and she had worried about all the fatty food she'd fed him over the years. Even her guilt couldn't be black and white, it seemed.

Lyda pricked her ears, but could hear nothing but the pounding on the front door. Sweat trickled down her back onto the curve of her hips. Her throat constricted, making it difficult to swallow as a pair of voices drifted into her range of hearing.

"I came by last night to pick up a few things and guess what? My keys didn't work. What makes you think you can change the locks on OUR house?"

"I was out of town on business. I didn't want you to come in here all hysterical, like you are now, and start breaking things. I'm sorry, officers, that you had to get dragged into this."

"You should be sorry, Nick. After I found out what you did, I had my lawyer get right on it. No one's going to keep me out of my own house."

"I'm afraid, sir, you're going to have to allow her to get her things," said a third voice that Lyda assumed was a cop's.

"Yolanda, you're the one who left in the first place. How was I supposed to know you'd want to come back," Nick protested angrily, his voice finally rising to the level of his enraged wife.

"Don't worry, Nick. I won't be here long. I'm just here to pick up my furs and my jewelry."

"No!"

The door to the closet was yanked open and Lyda found herself staring at a thirtiesh blond. Yolanda matched the decor perfectly, wearing a peach pantsuit, her medium length hair tied up in a teal bandana. There was no sense faking modesty at this point. Lyda let her hands fall to her sides. The color rushed from Yolanda's cheeks and her jaw dropped in a mixture of horror and disgust.

Lyda laughed, she couldn't help it. It figured that the only good time she'd had since her divorce had to turn into a public spectacle. The horrified look on Yolanda's face changed abruptly to one of stark hate. Yolanda's hand rose as if to hit Lyda, but then she whirled and began boxing her husband's ears.

"It looks like I had good reason to leave, doesn't it?" she screamed. "Doesn't it?" Nick tucked his head beneath the crook of his elbows like a boxer as Yolanda let him have it with both hands. The two mustached officers looked at each other in confusion, wondering if they should break it up.

Lyda mustered what remained of her dignity and threw on a silver mink from the closet. Without bothering to button, she ran to the side of the Jacuzzi, tossed her clothes and shoes into her overnight case, and made a beeline for the door. Yolanda jerked her head to the side and eyed what Lyda was wearing, and cuffed Nick with renewed enthusiasm.

"You better believe that coat's coming out of your half of the settlement, you son of a bitch," Yolanda hissed as Lyda shuffled past the police. She paused long enough to push down one of the locks on her case, and sprinted out the front door onto the finely manicured front lawn.

The grass was wet against her bare feet, still damp with morning dew. Lyda felt no sense of urgency as she made a long-legged dash toward the street. She flew across the green runway without fear or second guessing. Nothing would hurt her as long as she kept moving. Life is an emotional magnet, she thought, where you travel to and from those you love and who love you. An uncertain journey where the landmarks and boundaries change every bit as often as the destination.

THE POLICY

THE POLICY WAS AN ABERRATION for an office this size, they whispered in the lunchroom. The company underappreciated them: their verve, their resolve in the face of cheaper competition overseas, their passion to avoid layoffs with weekend hours and the appropriate head nodding when their assignments made no sense. How dare the management team place The Policy (printed double sided to save money) on their crappy chairs from Office Plus without warning? Some of them may have complained about the careless actions of their coworkers, but what about their rights to a reasonable work environment?

For starters, the 1960s office building was falling apart. Water stains in the corners of the meeting rooms were used by HR as a form of Rorschach during interviews. The fiberglass insulation panes in the ceiling buckled, revealing threadbare wiring. The bathroom made strange gurgling noises and you could overhear gossip from the opposite sex in the adjacent restroom. The windows were sealed and they had impeded views of palm trees and traffic because of company signage erected to be visible from the freeway overpass. They tattooed their cars and T-shirts with an ugly triangle logo intersected by a swirl. Their bonuses went to a company town car and driver, unused videoconferencing equipment, and executive sushi power lunches.

The bravest and laziest of them found the time and resolve to dissect The Policy, exposing loopholes, poorly phrased rules, gray areas to be exploited. *The company logo must be worn at all times.* Some of them with children knew about how to place temporary tattoos of the company on wrists, necks, and ankles. One of the recent college grads wore it as a bling necklace, and this led to bracelets, earrings, and belly rings with logos dangling. It was rumored that one of their graphic designers had hooked the emblem on a nipple ring, as The Policy did not state that the logo had to be visible…only worn.

No dating or cohabitation with other members of the office. This did not prohibit sexual relations, seemingly. Soon, the kitchen started smelling like coitus and burnt toast. Late hours were put in by some of them hoping to run into others in the supply room after seven PM, when non-corridor lights were turned off for cost savings. The CEO found condoms pulled over the handles of the company exercise equipment and demanded an immediate expansion of The Policy.

No pets on the premises. No one knew who got the idea to bring in the stray dog that the security staff adopted and kept in the parking garage. It had no nametags or owner, so The Policy was soon amended to say: *No pets or non-human mammals on the premises.* This led to their office lizard Toby, who lasted until The Policy Version 6 reached their chairs the following Monday.

No belly buttons visible led to stickers of logos placed over their innies and outies by some of the more in-shape staff wearing tank tops and cutoffs. *Only one framed photograph per workstation* helped proliferate photos of Hitler, Stalin, and Son of Sam. *You must share vendor gifts* spawned a shindig where a single bottle of red wine led to an epic game of late-night spin the bottle.

The Policy Version 8 was twice as long, but the loopholes kept being exploited by workers who had come to view themselves as exploited. Some of them stopped showering and shaving their legs. Others looked up swear words in dead languages to berate the management team during Wednesday morning walkthroughs. The Chief Innovation Officer demonstrated to the Executive Steering Committee in a PowerPoint bar graph how a head-on approach was a losing battle. Almost unanimously, they decided to give the best and worst of them a new assignment: to make The Policy so thorough that no one could exploit it to make the company look bad. A policy that would lead to no individuality and enhanced team performance. Their business was slow that month, so the CEO pitched an idea to the Board of Directors: they could sell The Policy to other companies. Even non-profits, schools, and government agencies could use a set of rules that made everyone focus on productivity in the exact same way. The anticipation of this bold new product led to rising stock prices and record executive bonuses.

A last few holdouts rebelled against The Policy Version 12 by singing answers to management to the rhythm of their favorite rock ballads and by passing gas during the all-staff meetings. The CEO cupped his ears and held his nose. It was time to break their communal spirit. The next version of The Policy contained a provision to punish workers for breaking rules that appeared in future versions of The Policy.

This, seemingly, did the trick. The workers followed the rules and bided their time. The Policy had winnowed their vocabulary to a thousand words and they all arrived, ate, evacuated their bladders, and worked in unison. They created audio, video, and binder version of The Policy, and translations for their international sales division. The Policy seemed unstoppable until the day one of them brewed a pot of coffee from the private stash of their CEO. The blend was from one of their competitors, and blatantly against The Policy. Rather than admitting that he himself had breached the rules, the CEO banned coffee in the office.

This was the final straw. Their Boston Harbor. Everyone, from the mail room to the board room, came to their senses and rebelled, destroying The Policy in every form: utilizing the shredder, computer viruses, and barbiturate binges to suck it out of their collective memories. This spread to their other offices around the world. The Policy could not survive this uprising in the place of its origin.

The CEO sometimes sat on the sink in the executive washroom, clutching the last copy of The Policy. The privilege to use this bathroom was his alone according to its edicts, but the riffraff had begun ignoring the old rules... and him. He slowly stripped away The Policy to create paper airplanes for protection, to defend his privilege. Eventually, the CEO tossed the pointy end of the rules into the eye of his assistant who came in to wash ink stains from her favorite shirt.

The next day, they all saw the victim wearing a pirate patch. Who would protect them against those in power? The office busybody whispered in the lunchroom: *we're not respected,* and raised to management in their next staff meeting that someone needed to create a policy against this type of behavior.

Outside

It wasn't one of those paltry blizzards in the lower 48 where the locals complain about the temperature dipping below zero. It was a November cold snap and hadn't been above minus 40 in over a week. A bit excessive, even for Fairbanks. Even in the hallway off my front parlor, I could feel icy air drilling the socks above my leather shoes.

"Hurry up," I yelled to Maureen, who was primping herself in the john off the hall. She'd left her car at the Golden Nugget and wanted me to drive her over to get it. Like most citified Alaskans—used to jumping from heated house to heated car—we weren't dressed for winter: no hat, no gloves, light coats. Our lack of clothes reeked of pioneer spirit, thumbing our noses at the harsh elements that ruled our lives. Not too bright...

"Christ, Paul, why do you have to get up so early?"

"Because I have a real job."

"Working for the government's real?"

"As real as Jesus."

"Cute," she said, applying lipstick in front of the brightly lit bathroom mirror. "Your father must be rolling in his grave."

"Urn."

I could see half a face glowing in the looking glass—lips pursed to receive a crimson shade, purple rings under eyes that had known too many late nights, and cheeks chapped by the dry cold. She dropped her make-up case into her purse and swung her ample hips into the hallway, closing the door. A dusky twilight bathed her dirty blonde hair from a storm window. She stepped through the shadowy hallway and stretched her arms, her half-lit outline statuesque in the dim corridor. At times like this, I could almost forget she was another man's wife.

******* ******* *******

Maureen paused in the icy driveway next to my old Dodge and pointed to a strange mound in my front yard. I squinted in the almost dark. The lump by the roadside could only be one thing...a terrible thing.

"It figures," she said. "Perfect start to a perfectly shitty day."

"I have a nine o'clock meeting. Think there's any way you can–"

"Not a chance. Clarence knows too many people on the force. The last thing I need is to start more rumors. Let someone else deal with it."

"I know the family, I think."

"Drop me off at the bar, OK? You can do whatever you want."

"Here," I said, sliding the ignition key off my ring, my fingers seared by the cold. "Take my car to the Nugget and I'll pick it up later."

"When did you become such a good Samaritan?"

Her icy words hung over the yard as my feet crunched the top layer of snow. The sky was dreary and the wind howled, stinging my eyes. I reached beneath the armpit of my blazer and felt for the comforting bulge of my .38 snug in its leather holster. It was nice to know my best friend was within arm's reach.

The ignition rumbled behind me and Maureen spun out of the driveway, spinning new powder onto the ditch separating my property from the road. I reached the oblong mound and noticed a cocktail dress scrunched in a pile next to bare feet spackled with frostbite. It was a native woman and she was naked, her eyelids frozen around two tiny coals, her normally ruddy skin blanched by the night's fierce snowfall. Her expression was frozen and faraway, two bottomless black pools where there had once been eyes.

******* ******* *******

By the time the ambulance arrived and carted off the corpse, I remembered the woman's name. Rosie something or other. My dad—a sourdough miner—had grown up in a Catholic orphanage with native kids, including Rosie's father. I had seen her around town quite a few times. Like many of the locals, she had a weakness for liquor. The paramedics figured she'd gotten drunk and tried to stumble home.

It wasn't uncommon for people suffering from hypothermia to strip off their clothes. After long exposure to subzero a person's arteries can burst, giving the illusion of unbearable heat. My own father, who used to fly his plane to his mine in Manley, crashed his Cesna three winters ago. Like many miners, he had already survived a number of emergency landings—five in all—but his legs were broken during this final crash. In the end, he took off his clothes and folded them next to him in a neat pile. That's the way the rescue team found him later that spring.

The look he'd had in his casket was the same one on Rosie when I found her: ecstatic, as though in the midst of an orgasm or a revelation.

It was closing in on eleven by the time I spoke to the cops, retrieved my car, and made it to the Department of Transportation. My staff noted my late arrival, but I figured they'd held the meeting without me. Cynthia, a wafer-thin brunette in her early twenties, approached my desk as I changed into a pair of dry shoes I kept there for emergencies.

"Are you OK?" she asked, eyes narrowing. "Some of us were hoping that something didn't happen to you on the road." She tossed her shoulder-length hair with a flip. "Some of us weren't."

It was just like Cynthia to be difficult when I felt least able to handle it. She smiled and drew fingers from imaginary holsters, firing away at me in staccato rhythm to her words, "Oh, and Blake wants to see you in his office."

She blew on her index fingers, turned and was gone before I could say a word, not that I wanted to explain anything to anyone, and especially not to her. I tucked the tail of my dress shirt into my slacks and laced my shoes before making my way to the lion's den. Blake's office wasn't called that because he was a hard ass, although he imagined himself one. It was because of the animals. The dead animals. Especially the bobcat mounted on the wall behind his desk.

He wasn't in when I entered, so I made myself comfortable, propping my feet on the sandalwood desk he'd imported from India. I stared at the animals and they stared at me. The heads of a moose and a bear rounded out the triumvirate of taxidermy, although if you looked closely at the matted fur you could see the gummed-up remains of price tags.

"Hi, Paul, glad you could make it," Blake said, shuffling into the room and closing the door behind him. He circled to his chair and eased his bulk onto a pillow. "I wanted to give you an update on *the incident.*"

The incident was Blake's code word for the sexual harassment lawsuit Cynthia had slapped on me.

"Because she's young enough to be your daughter and due to the severity of her accusations–"

I shot him a death look and Blake paused before continuing. I tuned him out. Most of the details I'd already heard. I kept glaring at him, slowing his bureaucrat's double-talk. I'd always thought I had the power of the evil eye. I had inherited the scintillating sea-green gaze of my Norwegian mother and could wield it like a weapon, one that had pierced through Cynthia. She'd given me the signs of interest: eye contact, laughing at bad jokes, brushing into me. My only mistake had been following up on her interest during a field trip to Nome and then ignoring her afterwards.

"So we think you should take vacation until the matter's settled," Blake finished with a flurry, uncomfortable with being the bearer of bad news. "Do you have anything more to say on the subject?"

"I'm a monster," I said, rising to leave, and even as I said it, I understood it meant nothing and everything.

******* ******* *******

My relationships with women continued its perfect record: 100% abysmal. I was destined to inflict pain on everyone who got close to me, even for a single night. What Maureen, Cynthia, and the others never understood was that I was doing them a favor by keeping them at arm's length.

I eased into the back lot of the Golden Nugget, parking next to a weather-beaten row of trucks and Outbacks. The numb was almost instantaneous as I connected the engine block of my Dodge to the complimentary outlets so the headbolt heater would stay running. I stumbled across the slippery driveway through the winter gloom that would soon devour almost all the sun for months to come. The back porch light was busted and it was a treacherous walk to the rickety staircase. The stars were shrouded in soot from a nearby plant and the only shadows were those I carried inside. The door opened to a back hallway next to a pay phone, cigarette machine, and bathrooms leaking light beneath their doors. I felt the pull of neon beer signs, the fluttering fluorescents above the pool table, and the red-lit jukebox just as my ancestors were drawn to the glitter of gold.

Inside the tiny main room, I paused and watched Maureen mix a cocktail behind the bar. She looked up at me, dropped a red straw inside the clear liquid, and swirled the plastic swizzle along the rim of the glass. She released the tip, dipped her hand into the back pocket of her jeans, and pulled out a ballpoint pen, massaging it with deft fingers.

I smiled and raised my eyebrows. A blast of hot air from a ceiling vent washed over my thinning hair. The phone behind Maureen rang and she turned to answer it, breaking her spell over me. I slicked down an errant tuft and hurried through the crowd to a small bank of tables out of sight from the bar.

Maybe going out wasn't such a hot idea. No amount of liquor was going to help me forget this pisser of a day. Although that didn't mean I wasn't going to give it my best shot.

"Hey, Paul, where you been?"

"Whose marriage you ruining these days?"

I recognized the voices. "Like your marriage wasn't already on the rocks," I said, looking into the amused faces of Rick Schmidt and Bill Mast, two boyhood pals and heavies in the local Republican Party.

"Ouch," Bill said.

Rick smiled, waving a bottle of Wild Turkey the paunchy pair had purchased from Maureen to save themselves the hassle of chasing down drinks.

"Been a long time, Paul." Bill said.

I had been avoiding them, but I motioned for them to

sit anyway. They were locals—Alaskans, like me. We preferred each other's company to the outsiders invading our homeland, even when we hated each other's guts.

****** ******* ******

The front door of the Golden Nugget slammed, rattling a wooden pegboard once used for mounting patrons' guns and holsters on the wall. I was rattled, too, feeling every bit as drunk as I must have looked to the few remaining regulars.

"I remember when you could leave your door unlocked," Rick said, thumbing a groove into the turkey's neck on the almost-empty whiskey bottle.

"Even when all the scum came up to work on the pipeline, they were making enough dough so that you didn't have to worry about your stuff getting ripped off," Bill shot back.

The bar's ancient jukebox flipped songs from one guitar-laden rock anthem to another. Rick and Bill were loud and getting louder by the shot glass. Ever since my wife left me to go back to America I'd fought my loneliness with politics, making cold calls for Republican candidates, editing the party's newsletter, carrying my message on business trips to the most remote native outposts.

Rick stroked his short beard. "It's those sons-a-bitches from the military bases."

Bill chuckled, but it sounded more like a chicken squawking beneath a farmyard ax. "They date our women, steal our cars, and take our welfare after they get discharged like it's their own country."

My throat constricted. A strange vision washed over me: Bill and Rick, naked and holding hands, lying in a snowdrift outside the bar. Happier than they'd been since childhood. I bolted up out of my seat and stumbled over my chair leg on the way to the bathroom, filled with a need I didn't understand.

"Hey, Paul, I remember when you could hold your liquor."

"You used to be one bad-ass stud, now...."

The world spun. Maureen winked at me from behind the bar. "Last call," she yelled. "Time to go home and cuddle up with something warm."

******* ******* *******

Warm, get warm, I told myself, tearing out of my clothes and diving into bed. I burrowed beneath the sheets and pulled the down comforter over me. I couldn't believe how stupid I was, taking a short cut across the frozen river. I was chilled to bone, but at least I'd told Maureen shove off. She can keep warm with that tonight.

I didn't love her, hadn't loved anyone since Samantha. Although it had happened over twenty years ago, the night she left me is still fresh in my mind, like snow too far north to ever thaw. She'd wrapped our two-year-old son James in a papoose of multicolored blankets. He'd had a cold bordering on pneumonia and had been crying throughout the night. I saw the suitcase at her feet and moved toward her. She said, "I'll scream if you touch me."

Man and wife, better or worse, sickness or health—these were the promises I thought formed the safety net beneath me when I confided my deepest secrets to Samantha, ones that made even me afraid. After much prodding from her one drunken winter night, I told her I had powers of the mind, like slowing my heart rate. She thought I was joking until I pressed her hand up to my chest and slowed the beating inside my rib cage to a crawl. She looked white, like I was going to croak, but I was intoxicated with liquor and pride, and told her how I could leave my body and travel to other places, other times.

My drinking had blurred even this moment of confession…of closeness with her. What should have been a moment of sharing turned to horror because of the monster she recognized within me. Samantha had looked at me with fear and stuck her fingers in her ears, telling me to shut up, that she would leave me, but the floodgates were open. "Babe, don't worry," I told her. "I have the power to curse people. Remember that shithead Frank who made your life miserable at work. Who do you think gave him that stroke exactly?"

She grew silent and rolled over, sobbing into the sheets. But everything I'd said was true. At least, I thought so at the time. People always say they want the truth, but they're just kidding themselves. They don't want to stare at honesty in the eyes every day, make love to it, and have it cradle their baby in the dead of night.

Tears rolled down my cheeks. The unfinished oak in the rafters of my bedroom spun like fan blades. Although I hadn't attempted it in years, I thought about trying to project myself from my body and trekking to visit James, Maureen, even Dawn, the woman I'd come closest to marrying after losing my family. I was too afraid to try...afraid that I was as crazy as Samantha must have thought me.

Dawn had come closest to melting through the wall of ice I surround myself with and waited five years for a question that never came, before leaving on a vacation to see her sister in Seattle—a visit that became permanent when she accepted a job there.

I fumbled through the snow-crusted clothes I'd thrown on the bed, gripping the handle of my pistol still fastened in its holster. It was my constant companion, truer than a dog or a wife. The wind gusted and slapped against the storm windows, swirling along the eaves with a howl that reminded me of a sick infant. An icy snowfall streamed onto the driveway. Winter had come to Fairbanks and would not be leaving any time soon.

****** ******* ******

Outside, the storm raged all week, picking up intensity. I'd managed not to leave my house since the fiasco at the Nugget, unplugging my answering machine and pacing the living room in my underwear. My first vacation in over a decade and this was how I spent it. Figures. I had a regimen of television to keep me company and an occasional trip to the woodpile in the garage to stoke my ancient furnace. For some reason I kept thinking about my father and the lessons he taught me about loneliness, diesel engines, and flesh as tough as leather. For so many years I hated the old man, and now with him gone all I could do was miss him, stupidly, without understanding why.

I wondered if James missed me, if he ever thought of me. When he was four, I flew down to see him in Spokane where Samantha had moved when she remarried. I stayed a week, watching him from afar from a car parked outside his home. At his nursery school, I watched how he flew away from the other children on the whims of his own private daydreams, much like I had been at that age.

I hatched an elaborate plan involving multiple rental cars, bought two one-way plane tickets to Fairbanks and, at the beginning of recess, plucked James from the nursery schoolyard from a hole in the chain-link fence I'd snipped the night before. He didn't scream or make a sound, although I could see he was frightened. To calm him, I told him I was daddy as I buckled him into the passenger seat and drove away. As we sped to where the next rental was parked I looked into his wide green eyes and told him we were flying to Alaska. James said, "No, daddy, I had a bad dream. Plane go down. Daddy go boom."

I don't know why this shook me up more than the fear of being charged with kidnapping, but it did. I turned the car around and dropped James back at the nursery school with no one the wiser. Frightened by my son's prescience, I ate the cost of the plane tickets and took the second rental car up the Alaskan highway. Now, years later, I wonder if James had seen his grandfather's death, instead of my own.

Beside me, the thermostat read 75°. I couldn't keep warm, even though I was sweating bullets. I slumped in my La-Z-boy and fumbled for a greeting card I'd been planning to send for weeks. I slid the card from its tan envelope, reread my message on the inside flap and returned it to its resting place on the coffee table. Not knowing what to do, I placed my .38 on top of it. A hell of a paperweight. Loaded and begging to be used.

****** ****** ******

"Good morning, Tommy."

My brother turned to face me on the porch of the house he'd built with his own hands. He had enough sense to close the front door behind him to seal in the heat before laying into me: "What in God's name are you doing out here in the cold?"

"Is that any way to greet your older brother?"

"Jesus, Paul, you could have knocked."

"I didn't want to wake you."

"I heard about your vacation."

"From…" I began, but Fairbanks was small on privacy, big on gossip.

"Didn't believe it at first," he said.

"What does that mean?"

"Means you're not the type to take time off and hang out at the homestead."

The little shit was right. He looked at me strangely, almost like he didn't know me. Not far from the truth. We were never close—he was a gold miner like my father.

"Look, Paul," he said, "Why don't you come in and have breakfast. Sarah and the kids are making some noise about pancakes. If there's something wrong, you can talk to us about it.

I was too used to playing the role of big brother to let him in on my problems. I'd spared him the details of how dad whipped me—and only me—with a belt growing up. It was then I started believing I had powers to fight back against the treacherous world of adults. It was then I started trying to leave my body to escape the pain.

"No thanks, Tommy."

"It ain't going to do you no good to go back home and stew."

He was right, but hanging out with him and his happy wife and kids wasn't going to cure what ailed me. Deep down, I knew what needed to be done, had known for years.

"Don't worry about me. I'm going *outside*," I said, using Alaskan slang for the lower 48. "It's been too long since I've been to America."

****** ****** ******

Outside it was overcast, but I'd driven far enough south to regain both sunrise and sunset. The drive through Canada was breathtaking, even as I found my throat constricting and had problems breathing the clean, crisp air. The top of the Rocky Mountain chain was interspersed with small alpine communities and glacier-fed lakes. It had been nearly a decade since I'd cruised the Alaskan highway. I used to fly down with my old man to Arizona when I needed a new car and drive it up with him from the states. We'd fight and laugh and swear and swill hard liquor as we motored back home. On the road, we were always more free with each other than we were on the inside, when he was constantly reminded that I was not a sourdough, not tough like him. Even Samantha had gotten along with him, recognizing something solid in him that she never saw in me.

My last trip to the states with my father was to see James. I had finally convinced Samantha to allow a supervised visit, but only with my father, whom she made promise that we wouldn't try to take him. Samantha wouldn't see me at all and James was at that difficult, closed-off age of fourteen. I don't remember a single remarkable passage between us during the entire day's visit. What stuck with me most was how much James reminded me of the old man. He had an aura of someone who was comfortable with people, with the earth. But instead of becoming a sourdough like he would have in Fairbanks, James's esteem was directed at his step-dad Mike, who owned a small apple orchard. Even with my own son, I was an outsider.

Next to me, the greeting card vibrated in the passenger seat from the rough stretch of two-lane north of Whitehorse. I was getting tired and would have to stop soon for the night. The occasional road kill along the shoulder seemed to be wearing smiles: a grinning raccoon, an ecstatic squirrel, teeth flashing from an indefinable mound of brown flesh. I listened to a garbled AM talk radio station and gauged the quality of road ahead. I'd worked for the Department of Transportation so long that the buckles, seams, and potholes pocking northern highways were more familiar to me than the contours of a woman's body.

My journey continued like an achingly familiar dream, as though I'd traveled this long stretch of road many times before. When I pulled off the road for gas or a place to spend the night, I wasn't in the mood for company. I avoided bars and roadside diners, ordering my meals through fast food windows.

I stopped only once and that was to help a family with a flat tire that had forgotten to pack the lug wrench on their trek north. The man seemed all right, if not a little out of his element. The wife looked at me warily, as though she could see through the half lies I was telling to feel like I had some measure of control. Her infant son stared at my eyes, his tiny hand reaching out to them. He could see that I was more like him than anyone he'd ever met: a creature yet to evolve, scared by a world he didn't understand. We were both immune to the import of words and gestures, banter about the weather and handshakes, thank yous and good-bye waves. We were outsiders to the world that swirled around us.

The last two nights I barely slept, and when I did, I dreamt that I was sprinting along a snow-covered road. The sun beating down on the icy landscape made me unbearably hot and I stripped off an article of clothing for each carload of families passing by—and they all were families, too, filled with husbands, wives, mother-in-laws, second cousins, grandmothers, and adopted uncles. Then I'd wake long before sunrise and race out to my car to continue the trip.

I cleared customs on the third morning and crossed the

border into the states, speeding toward Seattle. My old girlfriend Dawn lived in the suburbs there and I thought about the scattered invitations she'd mailed to me over the years. "No pressure," she stressed in her long, hand-written correspondences. I'd memorized her address, although I never sent back a reply. It seemed moronic to regret my decision five years after the fact.

Every impulse in my taut arms and shoulders screamed to take the on-ramp into Seattle, but my mission was clear. I got in the turn lane for I-90 and veered onto the eastbound interstate. I shifted in my seat and switched into the fast lane. My legs were stiff and the pit of my left arm had been rubbed raw by my shoulder holster. A road sign indicated 265 miles to Spokane. It was still well before noon. If I hurried I'd be able to make it there by nightfall.

****** ****** ******

I triple-checked the address on the now-creased envelope of my card before trekking to the front door of a dilapidated wooden farmhouse. I hadn't thought the outskirts of Spokane would be quite this rural. A cavalcade of cars and pick-up trucks in the gravel driveway made me pause, but I couldn't turn back now. I patted down my hair in the rearview and applied deodorant before heading toward a front porch littered with secondhand furniture that ran the length of the house.

I buttoned up my suit coat and thought about what I'd say. It was pleasantly nippy out: no snow or biting wind. Jagged pebbles and an occasional brown leaf from an enormous elm by the porch crunched beneath my shoes. A pull barn and tractor on the left side of the driveway were the only things that broke the horizon of clean-tilled fields, other than an occasional mound of hay glinting in the distance beneath the fading sun. Long thin shadows followed me up the porch steps, almost invisible, yet always with you…like death, like fatherhood.

Lights were on behind pulled shades in what I assumed was the living room. A rock song with heavy bass filtered through the front of the house. Not finding a doorbell, I rapped lightly with my knuckles. When there wasn't an answer, I balled my fist and pounded on a thick wooden panel. Just when I was about to give up, the door was wrenched open by a muscular blond in his early twenties.

"Come on, space case, you know it's unlocked," the youth said, before his jaw dropped. "Sorry, I thought you were someone else. Can I help you?"

Everything I'd thought about saying the last few days flew out the window. "I'm Paul your father. Happy birthday," I said, thrusting the card into his veiny hands.

"Thanks. I know who you are from the pictures you sent me. I just wasn't expecting to see you."

Both of us were equally at a loss for words. I could sense him making the same comparisons with old photos that I was. He'd filled out since college. He probably thought the same about me, although not in as flattering a way.

"What are you...twenty-three?"

"Twenty-four," he said.

Several silhouettes whisked by in the background. Light footsteps approached.

"You've got company. If this is a bad time, I can take off and-"

"No," he said, gripping my elbow. "We have unfinished business."

He motioned for me to enter and I ran straight into a young woman in a form-fitting cocktail dress. She had almost impossibly black skin.

"Sorry," I said.

"Latisha, this is my biological father. Paul, this is Latisha, my wife."

My heart froze in my chest and I tried to hide the look of shock that must have registered on my face. Latisha slapped James lightly across the chest with a solid backhand.

"Quit already. Enough teasing for today." She looked up at me with a warm smile. "We just got engaged and he's been telling that to everyone we've run into for weeks now."

"Oh," I said.

"James, I can definitely see the resemblance, especially

around the forehead. You've got wicked green eyes," she told me.

"Thanks."

"James has got 'em too. He thinks he can get away with anything with eyes like those."

"Damn near," James said, moving past the shock of my arrival and grinning from ear to ear.

"We're being rude. Won't you come in, Paul?" she asked.

I nodded and followed James through a small foyer into a cluttered living room brimming over with chip bowls, empty beer bottles and filled ashtrays. Laughter boomed from the kitchen. I caught Latisha making a gesture with her hand out of the corner of my eye. Don't get paranoid, I told myself and yet the movement was familiar. I'd seen my mother do it countless times growing up whenever she sensed an evil presence in her home.

******* ******* *******

I squeezed into an empty spot around the battered oak table in a combination dining room and kitchen, and was introduced to James' friends. Although the window above the sink was cracked, the room stank of cigarettes, take-out Thai, and the faint aroma of pot. I felt out of place and tried not to ruin the festive mood, but my conversation came out clipped, forced.

I found myself sweating bullets as I tried to make sense

of the movies and musical groups being discussed. I zoned out and found myself wondering what the young people around me would look like naked, with a neat pile of folded clothes at the foot of their chairs.

"So is Fairbanks anything like that town in *Northern Exposure*?" Latisha asked, moving the conversation from TV to something I could relate to.

"Afraid not, although I've seen some villages that aren't too far off. I never really watched the show."

"I hear it's a bitch to get satellite TV up there," said the bearded youth to my right who'd introduced himself as Paco, and the conversation turned toward the merits of high-definition television.

I felt like an outsider. Most of the guests worked or lived on-site in what I finally determined was a cooperative farm. I'd had no idea that James was capable of anything like this—he had studied chemistry in college and I thought he'd landed a job in the city.

James must have sensed my discomfort and suggested a walk. Latisha looked none too pleased about it since his birthday cake was next on the agenda, but he laughed and told everyone we'd be back soon. He grabbed a jacket and led me out the back door. He pointed toward a faint tree line in the distance and we stepped across the empty field in silence, toward the setting sun. The lengths of our legs uncannily similar, we strode in tandem, passing a half-dozen haystacks. I breathed in the crisp air. It was great to be outside in November. I'd spent too many falls and winters at home alone or else prowling brightly lit bars under jet-black skies for yet another conquest.

"Nice sunset," I said.

"Yep," he said and we continued walking toward the reddening horizon.

The silence was unbearable. I opened my mouth what seemed a hundred times, but couldn't form words. I wanted to tell him why I'd waited to visit him, that it wasn't because I didn't care. I'd been afraid that I would inadvertently curse his life or that he would pick up my rotten luck. Now, after so many wasted years, I didn't want to make James think that his old man was crazy.

But how far exactly was that from the truth?

He stopped us in the middle of the field not far from a scarecrow decked out in a bright blue disco jacket and filled with what appeared to be two-liter returnable bottles. He turned to me and asked, "Why are you here?"

"I'm not sure."

"Are you dying or something? It's the only thing I can think of that would make you come see me."

"I'm fine."

Anger rose in James's voice, "Really? Then it must be a mid-life crisis. I've been waiting for this to happen. What do you think, Dad," he said sarcastically. "We gonna be buddies now?"

"Look, I know I've been a rotten father."

"Damn straight."

"But you haven't made it any easier, you know?"

"Hey, I invited you to my graduation."

"And that's the only time you've ever written me."

"It's better than the card and check you send me every birthday."

I could feel my surrogate son—my gun—draw my hand towards it in my jacket pocket. Words came tumbling out, "I was trying."

"Pathetic if you ask me."

"We're strangers. That much is obvious. What kind of son gets engaged and doesn't tell his father?"

"The kind who doesn't have a father," he said.

"Sounds like I should leave then." I imagined a small hotel room and a big bottle of vodka, with me watching TV and cleaning my gun.

"Ahh Christ," James said, kicking at a small rock in the loose dirt. "Why don't we just make the best of this, huh?" James dug through his jacket pocket and pulled out a small clay pipe. "Wanna smoke a peace pipe?"

Another moment of silence passed between us and I wondered if James was trying to get under my skin or really wanted to bond with me. I couldn't read him, though, just as I never could my father when he invited me to go flying or mining or fixing the engine on his bulldozer. When the old man and I fought, we were miserable, but it was a shared misery. As close to love as men get.

James broke the silence by lighting his pipe and inhaling pungent marijuana smoke through the ornately carved mouthpiece. He offered it to me and seemed surprised when I helped myself to it. I'd been sober for three days now and figured it couldn't do any harm.

We passed the pipe back and forth, and I could tell he was getting less pissed off. A strange impulse washed over me. I reached for my handgun, loosening it from its holster. I pointed it away from James and asked, "Ever shoot one of these before?"

"You're kidding, right?"

"No."

"I don't much believe in guns."

"My dad taught me how to shoot a long time ago. Why don't you give it a try?"

James laughed so hard that he had to lean over, coughing. "Sure, a real father son moment," he said, gasping for air. "Why not."

I gave him the rudiments of handgun safety: how to always keep it pointed away from another person, where the safety catch was. I warned him about the kickback, too, but the recoil from his first shot at the scarecrow almost knocked him on his ass.

"Jesus, that's loud," he said. "Packs a wallop, too. Latisha's going to kill me for this."

I started laughing—I'm not quite sure why—and he joined me until we were both coughing and spitting up phlegm. James straightened and took aim at the scarecrow, planting his feet.

"Use both hands."

"Gonna get that ugly sucker," he said, squeezing the trigger of my .38 again and again, until there were only two shots left. He didn't come close to hitting it. He handed me the gun and I took aim, emptying the cylinder. If anything, I did worse.

"That was cool," James said. "Not sure it's going to be worth the tongue-lashing from Latisha."

"You can blame it on me. Tell her I'm out of my mind."

He laughed so hard this time that I thought he was going to cough up a lung.

"It's no joke, son. Your mother...."

"Told me about the break-up. In detail."

"Christ, I'm such an ass. You're being nice to an old man you don't know who decides to celebrate his son's birthday by dumping his problems on him."

"I'm kind of relieved you didn't come here acting superior."

"Why don't you keep it," I offered.

"What?"

"The gun."

"I'm not sure that's such a hot idea."

"I think it's probably a worse idea if I keep it.

"Maybe so, but–"

"Wait a second, I've got a better idea."

I double-checked to make sure the gun was unloaded and walked over to the scarecrow, fastening the weapon to the arm of its jacket. It took me a while to loop it so that it stayed fastened.

"How about that?"

"You're crazy, you know that?" James said as he came up behind me.

"Yeah, I do."

As the words passed my lip, I felt relieved. Maybe I wasn't destined to live my life as an outsider. The monster was unmasked, at least partially, and the villagers weren't after me with pitchforks. I looked at the trees waving to me in the distance and the last traces of sunlight disappearing behind them. I imagined myself flying toward the glow, toward Dawn in Seattle, and perhaps farther to family and friends in Fairbanks. In person, not in my dreams. I wasn't deluded enough to think the people I'd kept at arm's length would just flock to me, but I could tell them how I'd never wanted to leave my body when I was with them. I could tell my son things I could never tell my father.

"Not sure this changes anything," James said.

"I know."

"What now?" James asked, hands on hips. It suddenly struck me how much he looked like his grandfather when he was agitated.

"Not sure," I said. "I don't want to go inside quite yet."

"Me neither," he said and we walked aimlessly across the field until dusk gave way to night and we heard Latisha and James's friends calling to him from the house.

Fomite

A fomite is a medium capable of transmitting infectious organisms from one individual to another.

"The activity of art is based on the capacity of people to be infected by the feelings of others." Tolstoy, *What Is Art?*

Writing a review on Amazon, Good Reads, Shelfari, Library Thing or other social media sites for readers will help the progress of independent publishing. To submit a review, go to the book page on any of the sites and follow the links for reviews. Books from independent presses rely on reader to reader communications.

For more information or to order any of our books, visit
http://www.fomitepress.com/FOMITE/Our_Books.html

Nothing Beside Remains
Jaysinh Birjépatil

*The Way None
of This Happened*
Mike Breiner

*Summer on the
Cold War Planet*
Paula Closson Buck

*Foreign Tales of
Exemplum and Woe*
J. C. Ellefson

Free Fall/Caída libre
Tina Escaja

Speckled Vanities
Marc Estrin

Fomite

Off to the Next Wherever
John Michael Flynn

Derail This Train Wreck
Daniel Forbes

Semitones
Derek Furr

Where There Are Two or More
Elizabeth Genovise

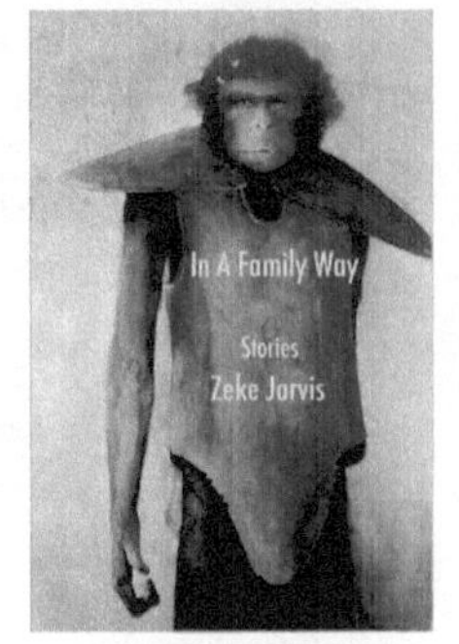

In A Family Way
Zeke Jarvis

A Free, Unsullied Land
Maggie Kast

Shadowboxing With Bukowski
Darrell Kastin

Feminist on Fire
Coleen Kearon

Thicker Than Blood
Jan English Leary

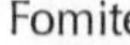

Fomite

*A Guide
to the Western Slopes*
Roger Lebovitz

*Confessions of a
Carnivore*
Diane Lefer

*Unborn Children of
America*
Michele Markarian

Shirtwaist Story
Delia Bell Robinson

Isles of the Blind
Robert Rosenberg

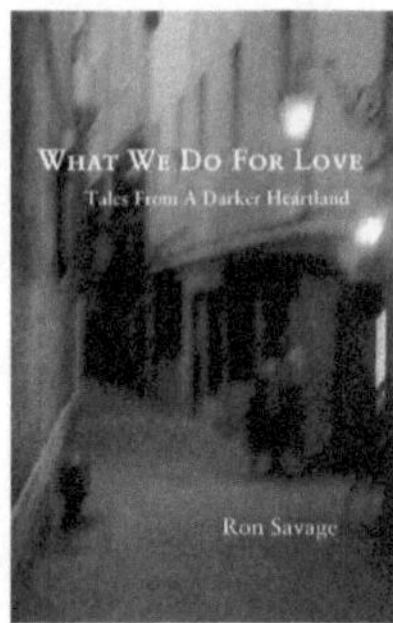

*What We Do For
Love*
Ron Savage

Bread & Sentences
Peter Schumann

*Planet Kasper
Voume 2*
Peter Schumann

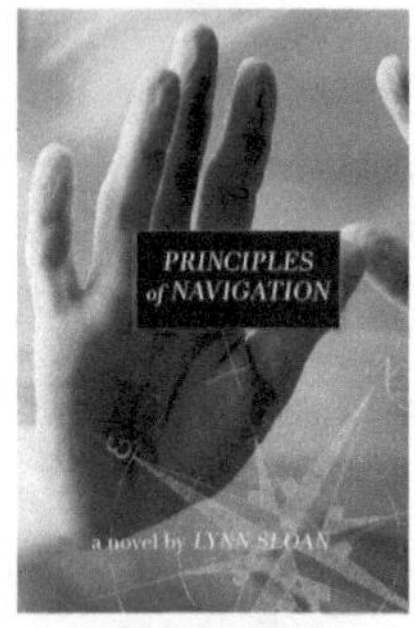

Principles of Navigation
Lynn Sloan

Fomite

Industrial Oz
Scott T. Starbuck

Among Angelic Orders
Susan Thoma

*The Inconveniece
of the Wings*
Silas Dent Zobal

Fomite

More Titles from Fomite...

Joshua Amses — *Raven or Crow*

Joshua Amses — The Moment Before an Injury

Jaysinh Birjepatel — The Good Muslim of Jackson Heights

Antonello Borra — Alfabestiario

Antonello Borra — AlphaBetaBestiaro

Jay Boyer — Flight

David Brizer — Victor Rand

David Cavanagh — Cycling in Plato's Cave

Dan Chodorkoff — Loisada

Michael Cocchiarale — Still Time

James Connolly — Picking Up the Bodies

Greg Delanty — Loosestrife

Catherine Zobal Dent — Unfinished Stories of Girls

Mason Drukman — Drawing on Life

Zdravka Evtimova —Carts and other stories

Zdravka Evtimova — Sinfonia Bulgarica

Anna Faktorovich — Improvisational Arguments

Derek Furr — Suite for Three Voices

Stephen Goldberg — Screwed and other plays

Barry Goldensohn — The Hundred Yard Dash Man

Barry Goldensohn The Listener Aspires to the Condition of Music

R. L. Green When You Remember Deir Yassin

Fomite

Greg Guma — Dons of Time

Andrei Guriuanu — Body of Work

Ron Jacobs — All the Sinners Saints

Ron Jacobs — Short Order Frame Up

Ron Jacobs — The Co-conspirator's Tale

Kate MaGill — Roadworthy Creature, Roadworthy Craft

Tony Magistrale — Entanglements

Gary Miller — Museum of the Americas

Ilan Mochari — Zinsky the Obscure

Jennifer Anne Moses — Visiting Hours

Sherry Olson —Four-Way Stop

Andy Potok — My Father's Keeper

Janice Miller Potter — Meanwell

Jack Pulaski — Love's Labours

Charles Rafferty — Saturday Night at Magellan's

Joseph D. Reich — The Hole That Runs Through Utopia

Joseph D. Reich — The Housing Market

Joseph D. Reich — The Derivation of Cowboys and Indians

Kathryn Roberts — Companion Plants

David Schein — My Murder and other local news

Peter Schumann — Planet Kasper, Volume Two

Fred Skolnik — Rafi's Tale

Lynn Sloan — Principles of Navigation

L.E. Smith — The Consequence of Gesture

Fomite

Fomite

www.ingramcontent.com/pod-product-compliance
Lightning Source LLC
Chambersburg PA
CBHW061537210726
48287CB00006B/1987